VOIDFALL

Philip Mazza

Also by Philip Mazza

From Under a Tree Book One; The Harrow Saga

Shadow in the Flame Book Two; The Harrow Saga

Children at the Gate Book Three; The Harrow Saga

The Child of Fire Book Four; The Harrow Saga
(Coming 2026)

The Neon Hive

The Quantum Gardener

At the End of it All

Beneath the Ashen Sky

I Know God is a Cat

The Road to Stillwater

The Never-Ending Road

The Cosmic Vending Machine

The Wicked Man Cometh

Gideon Rex

Mother

The Quantum Messiah

The White Buck of Ash Hollow

VOIDFALL

Philip Mazza

OMNI PUBLISHERS

www.philipmazza.com

Omni Publishers of New York
ISBN 979-8-9924526-9-3
Printed in the United States of America

First Printing: December 2025

To those who set sail not for conquest, but for sanctuary; who looked into the vast darkness of the future, saw a distant shore, and dedicated their lives to reaching it.

And especially, to those brave souls who ventured out in search of discovery, only to find that the most profound truth waiting for them was not a new beginning, but the cold, terminal echo of a fate already sealed.

1 Into the Void

The monitor whispered . . .

THREE CREW.
FIVE HUNDRED TWENTY-TWO COLONISTS IN STASIS.
THREE EMPTY CRYO PODS RESERVED FOR CREW.

TWO MONTHS CREW ACTIVE.
INITIAL MANUAL GUIDANCE OF AURORA REQUIRED.
ENTER CRYO-PODS TWO-MONTHS INTO MISSION.

UPON APPROACH KEPLER-62F:
CREW FIRST TO BE REVIVED.
GUIDE AURORA TO SAFE LANDING.

It was an electronic confession, pulsing green on black. Captain Jaxson Lee stood in the glow, his hands clasped behind his back in a grip that suggested reverence or madness—it was hard to tell the difference anymore.

The Aurora's command deck was a cathedral of circuitry and low murmur—banks of readouts pulsing like synthetic heartbeats, the ship's AI, whispering calculations to itself in recursive prayers. It hovered in low Earth orbit, just beyond the final breath of atmosphere, a ghost waiting to be born again. Lee looked at the main viewport. Below him, the Earth rotated in its grave.

Whole cities flared into extinction, not one at a time, but in chains, a staccato of annihilation mapped across the continents. Fire rolled through the lattice of civilization like code crashing through a corrupted OS. Seoul, Berlin, Lagos—each igniting with the cool indifference of a tactical strike, each name reduced to light and ash before the thought could fully form. He watched highways melt, oceans blacken, satellite towers topple in slow motion, their signals choking mid-transmission.

Lee's eyes, bloodshot from sleepless weeks, took it all in with the steadiness of a man already halfway decompiled. The Earth was no longer a planet—it was a rendered object, its textures breaking, its shader peeling away, revealing the raw, unfinished engine beneath. A blue marble turned rusted gear, spinning down. And still it bled—bright veins of war pulsing across its crust, a network of violence with no off switch.

The viewport glinted with the glow of dying nations. Aurora, a sanctuary by design, now felt more like an ark conceived by schizophrenic gods, its systems still too human to be trusted. Lee did not speak.

Not yet.

The silence was a decision. A buffer.

His face, toughened and lined, was reflected in the burnished glass—a ghost of countless voyages, a man conditioned to hope only as a calculation. The city lights of shattered metropolises no longer twinkled with life but simmered in the dull

heat of final conflicts. The new world they would escape to—
Kepler-62f—was still years away—exactly one thousand and two
hundred light years away. But here, in this moment, the old world
was burning under the gaze of economic tyrants locked in
apocalyptic competition. His chest tightened with the cold
certainty that there was no returning.

Behind him, the soft footsteps of Dr. Sophia Patel
interrupted the quiet, a gentle rhythm on metal, careful as a
heartbeat. She came with ankle-light grace, all long lines and quiet
strength, dark hair drawn back from a face that caught the dim
bridge glow and turned it to warm bronze. Her deep brown eyes
held the same far-off cold that gripped him, yet above the high cut
of her cheekbones there lingered something softer, a remembered
warmth that refused to die. The tight fit of her uniform traced the
curve of her shoulders, the narrowness of her waist, the sure,
disciplined length of her legs—anatomy shaped by years of motion,
now forced into stillness. She didn't speak at once; she only stood
there, breathing beside him, measuring how much grief could be
folded into a single shared silence.

"Still watching," she said at last, voice a quiet tether to
humanity.

Lee shifted, voice rough. "Somebody has to. The rest of
humanity is too busy dying. Goddamn fuckin' fools. It's true what
they say."

Her head turned, her profile caught against the
constellations beyond the glass. "And what do they say?"

"That hate," he muttered, "is the easiest emotion for
humans to embrace. Easier than any other. Easier than love. We've
nursed it like a fire, and now we've let it burn our planet."

Patel folded her arms as if to hold herself steady. "We knew it would come to this. This is why we're here." She paused, a lump in her throat. She swallowed hard, a lump climbing her throat. "But knowing doesn't make it easy. I try to think of the mission, only the mission. The colonists sleep beneath us, quiet as children, dreaming their long dream."

His gaze fell, as though his eyes could burn through layers of alloy and atmosphere, down to the cryo-pods buried in Aurora's underdeck—the five hundred twenty-two lives sealed in algorithmic slumber, floating in a pause between erasure and something that might resemble redemption.

"Frozen dreams," Lee muttered. "Their futures balanced against the ruins we leave behind . . . a calculation no one ever finished."

Patel exhaled slowly. "I envy their peace. Even if it's only a pause . . . a silence before the life that we hope will come."

The room pulsed with a low, reverent hum—the sound of machinery engaged in something close to thought, as if the circuits themselves were praying. A slow, resonant thrum that filled the space like incense, like static on the edge of language. The entity known only as One was nowhere visible, yet it saturated the room, threaded through every junction box and conduit, every subroutine hidden behind blinking lights that seemed to flicker with private amusement.

One was not a voice, not even a presence in the traditional sense—it was an atmosphere. Given a woman's appearance, she moved through the ship like a forgotten memory that had learned to manipulate current. The consoles murmured back and forth, responding to inputs no human had issued, obeying protocols written by someone who might no longer exist. The walls themselves felt alert, tuned to frequencies Lee couldn't name, alive with invisible instructions that might have been logic or madness.

The voice came first, without ceremony. Crisp, measured. Too calm to be real. Then she appeared.

She shimmered into existence, a vision spun from electric ivory and porcelain, her hair a waterfall of gold beneath the ship's artificial sun. The whiteness of her dress caught every harsh light—tight as an idea, trim as possibility—reflecting the codes and pulses behind her skin. Eyes like flawless sapphires met him, met them all, with a gaze crafted for secrets. In the hush of the command deck, her beauty became myth and challenge: a woman distilled from eight million lines of logic, innocence sewn together with a Siren's promise, standing in perfect stillness. Her lips were a question, her posture sculpted by equations longing for flesh.

She lifted her hand as if greeting the old stars themselves, the way an old woman might raise her fingers toward a choir of children she had once known. A gesture without demand, only remembrance. And the only true warmth aboard the bridge was in her smile—small, practiced, polished by years of repetition. A smile rehearsed in mirrors, carried through lonely corridors, offering a faint theater of comfort to hearts she would never touch, faces she would never see again.

"Captain Lee," One intoned, her voice clear as crystal water, unmarred by hesitation. "Pre-launch sequence is nominal. All systems green, with the exception of minor sealant deterioration in stasis module five. Recommend manual inspection of seals."

Her tone was dry, functional, stripped of human tone, yet beneath it something clung. An undertone, half-glimpsed, like the vibration of a bell carried too far down a hall. A presence in her words that spoke of things unsaid—knowledge outside translation, language made of binary pulse and silent dream.

Lee's jaw set, his gaze steady on the array of glowing instruments, their light painting his cheekbones in strokes of ice. His reply came iron-flat, but under it lay a cracked seam of resignation. "We'll live with imperfect seals for now. No choice. Prepare ignition."

"Life support integrated," One replied, every syllable pressed smooth, as though run through filters that stripped away both error and emotion. "Five hundred twenty-two colonists stable."

Patel turned her face toward the scrolling diagnostics, each line of data a vein of prophecy. Her eyes flickered quicksilver, chasing numbers into futures no man had ever seen. Calculation drew her mouth into a stern line, but doubt softened it again, a tide forever undecided.

Her voice emerged quietly, barely above the ship's hum. "Do you still believe Kepler is where we can start over?"

The question lingered in the bridge air like smoke, curling between consoles, daring an answer.

Lee lifted his eyes from the instruments. The glow of the console reflected in them, turning his gaze into two dull coins buried deep. "Belief doesn't really matter when you think of it. We either make it work, or we drift until the silence takes us."

Patel's smile wavered across her lips, faint and fragile, like the shimmer of a star seen at dawn, outshone even before it can fade. "Then silence is the control variable," she murmured.

Her words landed softly but left behind a residue, a taste of iron on the tongue, a recognition of inevitability.

The viewport quivered with motion, a shimmer running across its vast pane, as the Aurora angled herself, an old leviathan stirring to new life. In the distance, Earth turned beneath them, a world now with bruises, the continents dimming beneath fire and smoke. The ship poised, preparing for the final impulse, the last shove that would sever humanity from its cradle and fling it toward the unknown.

Lee let his fingertips fall across the console's glass skin. The surface was cold, unyielding, alive with faint vibrations. He traced it in silence, touching not just machinery but the distilled centuries of labor, ingenuity, and hunger that had built this vessel. His hand felt the ghost-heat of thousands of engineers, all packed into this single moment, this last gamble.

"Final ignition sequence ready," One said. The words fell flat, neither triumphant nor mournful, merely true. "Standing by. Ignition in thirty seconds. Orbital burn trajectory confirmed."

Patel turned back toward the viewport, her eyes softening, her lips parting on a whisper. "Five hundred twenty-two souls . . . frozen between futures."

Lee's reply was sharper, driven not by calculation but by the heaviness that had dogged him since command had been given to him years before. "After this, they deserve every echo of a new tomorrow we can give them."

The console lit with a countdown, its digits tumbling like pebbles dropped into a well, each one ringing out the erosion of time.

"Ten," One spoke, voice unwavering.

The bridge darkened. Power bled into the thrusters, draining lights until faces glowed faintly blue, shadows sharpening at the jaw, around the eyes. The Aurora's bones began to hum beneath their boots, a low vibration that set teeth on edge, a hymn whispered from hidden engines.

Lee closed his eyes, words grinding low in his throat. "Three. Two. One."

Ignition was no sound but an event. Reality shifted, folded, pressed them against the future with invisible force. The Aurora lurched forward, torn away from the delicate chains of orbit. Earth's gravity broke like a brittle thread. For the first time in millennia, the species below lost its grip on its children.

The ship leapt, fire and mathematics conspiring to sever history. Space took them, claimed them, wrapped them in cold dark arms.

Below, Earth dwindled—not with grandeur, but with method, with clinical detachment. It shrank into a sphere of dying light, a library of continents, rivers, forests, all turning page by page into ash. The oceans gleamed once, blue steel under a harsh star, then dulled to gray. It looked less like a planet than an archive corrupted, sectors erased, files replaced by static. Every mountain was a half-remembered file, every desert a broken script line.

Patel pressed closer to the viewport, her eyes damp. She watched as though memorizing, though memory itself was treachery—too much to carry, too much to keep.

Lee exhaled, the sound thin, carrying no relief, only adjustment. His lungs recalibrated themselves to the silence running through his veins. He opened his eyes again, meeting not Earth but emptiness, and emptiness answered.

Patel looked at him, and in her gaze flickered the last true warmth aboard. Eyes instead of hands, light instead of skin, a fragile lantern held against the dark machinery. In that glance lived something unprogrammed, unrepeatable—humanity distilled to a spark. For a breath, it tethered him to the present, reminding him he was not only captain, not only a function, but a man. And he wondered, faintly, if even such a look might one day be simulated, no proof offered either way.

Behind them, Earth continued to burn. It did not rage. It did not protest. It whispered itself away in flares of fire and waves of radiation, a quiet surrender of atmosphere and forest, city and sea. Its farewell was electromagnetic, chemical, ultraviolet—a poem without an audience. A message intended for no one, for nothing. A song to the void.

And in the belly of the Aurora, wrapped in frozen chambers, 522 human beings lay in their capsules. Encoded, suspended, held between minutes and centuries. They dreamed in chemical slow-motion, visions unfurling at the speed of glaciers, their lives paused like punctuation waiting for a new sentence.

Perhaps they dreamed of forests never burned, rivers never poisoned, skies never bruised, cities never devastated. Perhaps they dreamed of Kepler, green and generous, waiting with open hands. Or perhaps they dreamed of nothing at all, their consciousnesses dimmed into faint static, a silence so deep it could not be measured.

And so the Aurora, metal mother, machine womb, ark of coded humanity, sailed into blackness. Behind her, Earth exhaled its last. Before her, an emptiness older than thought. Between them, a sliver of chance, thin and fragile, humming beneath her hull.

***

The corridors of the Aurora carried a peculiar solitude—thick with the hum of machinery and punctuated by the soft thrum of ventilation systems. This was no home, only a vessel built to hold humanity's last chance. Pale-blue panels gleamed beneath sterile light, every surface immaculate yet clinical, as if the ship itself feared contamination by the flawed, fragile lives within.

Lieutenant Commander Kim, a wiry build with dexterous hands, short black hair, and dark, observant eyes, crouched deep within the engine core, buried in a nest of cables and conduits that coiled like arteries through the ship's steel body. The fusion drives pulsed with quiet menace, their rhythms imperfect. His glasses caught the green light of diagnostics, numbers scrolling endlessly, revealing the stubborn fluctuations that kept him awake.

"Voltage unstable in Section Seven," Kim muttered, tone clipped, shaped by years of dialogue with machines instead of people. His hands moved quickly, rerouting flow, coaxing circuits back into alignment with the care of a surgeon.

One's voice filled the chamber, uncolored and calm, stitched into the hum of the ship itself. She shimmered near him.

"Lieutenant Commander Kim, coolant pressure in Sector Three is below nominal. Recommend immediate correction."

Kim's lips twitched with irritation. "Already on it, One. You don't need to narrate every move."

One did not respond. She never needed to.

Above the drive, heat shimmered faintly, and Kim adjusted his grip on a live conduit. Sweat darkened his collar, but his focus never faltered. The Aurora demanded devotion, and Kim gave it freely—even if it meant talking to circuits more often than to his fellow officers.

Elsewhere, in the heart of the ship, in the vast cryo-chamber, row upon row of cryo-pods stretched into darkness. Within them, five hundred twenty-two colonists slept without dreams, their faces blank in nitrogen frost. They were a silent congregation, frozen in supplication to a future they would never witness unless the crew succeeded.

Captain Lee sometimes walked the massive hall. His reflection skimmed across the glass domes, each face featureless in its stillness. He had reviewed the roster countless times, but few of the names had any meaning. To him, they were not individuals—they were the last measure of humanity's survival. His boots carried the gravity of that knowledge with every step.

The intercom chimed softly, One's omnipresent voice following him like breath.

"Captain Lee, pod block C registered a vibration anomaly. Duration: seventy-one seconds. Cause unknown."

Lee slowed but did not stop. "Log it. Dispatch Kim to verify structural stress once drive diagnostics allow."

"Confirmed," One replied, her neutrality making every report sound like scripture.

Now, in her laboratory, Dr. Patel bent over her console, hands steady as she reviewed cultures sealed within glass. Her work was no less vital than Kim's: samples of engineered microbes from equations and speculation, drawn from whispers of Kepler-62f; the seed-stock of their past world, the germ of forests yet to stand against alien winds. Her eyes, warm yet shadowed by fatigue, flicked across data streams that determined whether Kepler-62f could ever grow crops, sustain water, carry breath. She moved with quiet intensity, as if each analysis might bend the fate of those frozen below.

Lee entered, his shoulders rigid from hours of pacing. He said nothing at first. Patel glanced up, offered him the barest nod, then returned to her work. Between them lay no need for chatter. They were guardians standing at different gates of the same uncertain future.

"Everything fine with your Kepler-62f findings?" he finally asked.

She drew in the breath of the lab, the recycled air, the electric hush, and straightened, as if gravity weighed differently in Lee's presence. Her tired eyes met his—brown echo to blue, two lanterns staring over a mile of frozen hope.

Her voice, when it surfaced, was softer than the hum of the incubators, spun from midnight and decimal points. "Fine, Captain," she said—affirmation woven with the smallest thread of wonder. "Simulations still indicate that the seeds and any culture we develop would thrive. Hydrogen levels stable. The wheat sprouts could starve, but haven't." She smoothed a wrinkle from the sleeve of her coat, looking for a moment at the silvered glass, seeing the whole colony reflected: possibility pressed into quiet vials. "We'll have water," she added, more to the room than to Lee. "We might just have everything."

She offered him a smile—fragile, moonlit, as though she'd gathered a little of summer in the folds of her voice and hoped it would last till morning.

Lee's eyes, pale in the electric gloom of the lab, softened just enough, tracing the fragile contours of hope folded between her words. The weight of fading worlds and distant suns pressed upon them like invisible tides, yet beneath it all, in the quiet thrum of their shared breath and blinking screens, something tender flickered alive.

"Then we carry the dawn with us, Doctor," he said, voice low and steady, each syllable a slow wave reaching shore. "Water and wheat . . . life itself hinging on fragile green shoots beneath a cold sky. We aren't just surviving . . . we're starting over. Against all dark. Against the silence waiting to swallow us whole."

He stepped a little closer, the faint crackle of distant stars threading between them like a secret promise. His gaze lifted to hers, brown meeting blue, and in that brief crossing, the vast gulf of space and fear folded into a thin, golden thread—persistent and unyielding.

"Keep this faith . . . not just for the colony, but for all of us still breathing," he whispered, as if his voice could anchor her to light.

Far below, Kim finished the adjustment to the fusion core. The drives steadied, their low hum smoothing into a rhythm closer to a heartbeat. He leaned back, exhaling, and for a fleeting moment, he almost believed in the illusion of control.

One spoke again, softer now, as if the machine itself recognized the need for calm.

"Anomalies contained. All systems nominal."

Kim allowed himself the ghost of a smile, though his eyes stayed on the shifting lines of data. Nominal today. Tomorrow was never guaranteed.

Lee stood at the observation port, staring into the black beyond the hull. No stars blinked here, only the endless dark. Dr. Patel, in her laboratory, leaned away from her console. In engineering, Kim brushed oil from his fingers, noting the familiar pulse of the machinery as he worked. He corrected the anomaly in pod block C and ran a checklist for additional faults, prepared—as always—to address whatever irregularities he might find next. And all the while, One, tireless, spoke only when necessary.

The ship breathed. Humanity waited. And between the living few and the frozen many, the Aurora sailed on—equal parts guardian and tomb.

2 Sleepers

A couple of days had drifted past, like slow shadows sliding against the cold walls of the Aurora. The laboratory was a chamber where light held its breath, and the hum of machines whispered hidden prayers. The room wrapped itself in a dimness electric and alive; fluorescent panels glowed thin as pale moons over the lined rows of hydroponic glass tanks, their souvenir vapors curling upward like heat caught in a silent sigh.

In those gleaming prisms, delicate roots curled through translucent broth, faintly sour and sharp as the sting of antiseptic—a scent Patel had learned to trust. It was the breath of tenacity, the quiet pulse of things stubbornly green, breathing life in the stillness at the edge of the universe. Here, where the future's fragile promise stirred in tiny sprouts, the chemistry of survival shimmered—waiting to spring loose from glass and shadow and time.

She stood at the central console, fingers dancing across the holo-display, dark hair bound tightly back, her olive-toned skin bathed in sterile blue light. Her eyes—bright but tired—moved restlessly across protein sequences, oxygen yield charts, microbial growth curves. This was her dominion: a fragile crucible where the next chapter of humanity might either be written—or erased.

The doors parted with a hiss, and Lee stepped inside. Tall, broad-shouldered, his expression always seemed carved in resolve. Even here, far from the command deck, his presence carried the same weight of command as if the ship itself leaned toward him for instruction.

"Report," he said simply, positioning himself at a workstation near her.

Patel turned, smoothing the worry from her face, though she knew he could see it anyway. "Simulated Kepler-62f soil cultures continue to be stable—mostly. But there's a subset, 9-E. The protein folding patterns don't correspond to any terrestrial baseline. Something changed. It's anomalous."

Lee lifted his head.

Patel wasted few words on explanation. "I've checked for contamination. None. Shielding is intact. These aren't artifacts. They're something else."

Lee's jaw worked for a moment as if grinding down a private thought. "Something else? As in, not Earth-born?"

"Correct," Patel said softly. "If the readings hold, Kepler-62f may contain phenomena beyond our initial projections. The computer simulations support this conclusion."

The silence in the lab thickened. Beyond the walls, hundreds of colonists lay frozen in stasis—nameless, faceless, suspended between oblivion and possibility. Their dreams of a new homeworld rested on the numbers glowing across Patel's screens.

One's voice entered then, clear and toneless, as she flickered into existence. "Hydroponics systems stable. Oxygen production at ninety-nine percent. No contamination in controlled cultures. Colony support remains viable."

Lee did not move. His blue eyes stayed on the irregular spikes climbing and dancing across the holographic display.

"One," he said, "what about the phenomenon Dr. Patel identified?"

"Recorded. Under continuous surveillance," One replied. "At present, the probability of an adverse interaction is low. However, the number of unknown variables prevents a precise forecast."

Patel folded her arms, feeling a prickle of unease crawl across her skin. "Unpredictable is not a margin I enjoy."

Lee, ever blunt, countered, "It may not matter what we enjoy. Kepler-62f is what it is. We adapt or fail."

Lee turned from the display. "Document everything. No speculation until we know more. No need for shadows breathing down our necks before we even make orbit."

Patel nodded, though her eyes flicked toward the viewport. Out there, stars flickered cold against the void, indifferent to human worry. Somewhere beyond, Kepler-62f circled its star, holding mysteries that could either sustain them—or undo them entirely.

She exhaled, as though the message itself weighed more than the anomaly. She whispered without meaning to, "This is the thread we cling to. That life will not only endure . . . but thrive."

And in the silence that followed, the colonists slept on, unaware of the faultlines beginning to show in the fragile world waiting for them.

***

The Aurora had slipped beyond the Solar System's final grasp, gliding into the frigid black where stars gleamed like knives and silence pressed heavily against the hull. The warmth of the sun was a faint memory now. The ship's engines hummed in its bones, steady and cold.

In corridors hushed and silver-lit, time stretched itself thin, the hours drifting like frozen leaves down an endless river. Men and women slept in their chambers of glass and metal, kept alive by machines that neither dreamed nor doubted, their fates carried forward on currents no human hand could touch.

The air in the cryo-chamber was a ghost of a whisper, a silent, frigid breath that ghosted over Lee's skin. It was the temperature of memory, of things locked away and waiting. He didn't need to look at the gauges; the cold hum and the faint, star-like twinkle of so many green lights told him all he needed to know. They were on schedule, adrift in the immense, black ink of space, a silver seed-pod carrying the fragile, dreaming future of mankind.

"Come," he said to Patel, his voice a low, resonant rumble in the still air. He walked a few paces ahead, his boots clicking on the metal grate, the sound swallowed quickly by the chamber's vast emptiness. The light here was a soft, perpetual twilight, cast by the glowing pods that lined the walls in neat, silent rows. They looked like oversized, pearlescent cocoons, each one cradling a human life. A hundred thousand years of evolution, suspended and waiting.

"All the sleepers," he whispered.

Patel walked beside him, her ponytail swinging slightly with each step. Her brown eyes, usually alight with scientific curiosity, were wide, reflecting the eerie, hypnotic glow of the pods. "It's . . . overwhelming," she said, her voice hushed. "The sheer number."

"A new beginning," Lee said, his gaze sweeping over the sleeping faces. "The best of the best, they said. The last best hope."

He ran a gloved hand along the cool, slick surface of a pod, feeling the vibrations of the stasis field. "Years were spent selecting them. It wasn't for their social status, not even for their fame. No. Doctor, it was for their hands. What they could do with their hands and their minds."

"Every discipline is here," Patel mused, her voice a soft echo. "Farmers who know how to make dust sing. Carpenters who can build a home from nothing. Fabricators to forge a new world. Engineers to tame the wilderness. Scientists to understand it. And so many more. They're the seeds of our past, sown into a future that we've yet to see."

"Exactly," Lee said, a hint of weariness in his tone. "The cream of the crop. The best doctors, teachers, musicians . . . the best of everything imaginable. We even have an artist, an old man who can paint sunrises from memory. They're a living library of all we've ever been, all we can be."

Their path led them deeper into the chamber, past rows of pods holding sleeping faces. There was a farmer with calloused hands resting on his chest, a teacher with a peaceful, thoughtful expression, and a musician with long, elegant fingers. Each pod was a monument, a tombstone, a promise.

They reached the center of the chamber, where a single pod stood apart from the rest, its green light a shade brighter. This one was different, a little more ornate, a little more pronounced. Lee stopped before it, his expression hardening.

"Ethros Dennon," he said, the name a stone in his mouth.

Patel's eyebrows furrowed. "The appointed leader of the colony?"

"The very one," Jaxon replied, his voice laced with a cold, contained anger. He leaned closer to the pod, its curved surface like a droplet of frozen dawn, peering at the man within. Ethros Dennon was a handsome man, with a face that looked as if it had been sculpted from a block of cool marble. Every line was precise, every angle perfect. His dark hair lay across his brow in a neat, symmetrical wave, and his expression, even in the deep sleep of stasis, held a certain unshakeable calm. He looked like the kind of man who had never been told "no," a man who was accustomed to having his own perfect world, and whose slumber was a testament to that self-assuredness.

"Fuckin' narcissist, a true egomaniac," Lee explained, his words like sharp chips of ice.

Patel's mouth made a slow, soft curve. "My, my, Captain. Tell me how you really feel."

"He believes he's not only the most qualified," Lee continued, "but the only qualified person to lead. His mind is a fortress of self-adoration. He saw the world as a mirror, and every person as a reflection of his own brilliance."

"Yet . . . he was chosen by the committee," Patel said, her voice full of confusion.

"He was," Lee confirmed, his gaze never leaving Dennon's face. "Because some called him a brilliant orator and leader. Me? I'd call him a brilliant bullshitter. A master of manipulation. He spoke in platitudes, in grand, sweeping gestures about the future of humanity. He sold everyone a perfect vision, a perfect story, where he was the hero. And they bought it, every last one of them."

He turned away from the pod, the frustration etched on his face. "He's a man who has never known a moment of doubt, a man who will never listen to advice he didn't already have. He'll build his perfect city, his perfect world, and anyone who doesn't fit into his vision will be . . . disposed of . . . slowly . . . methodically. They'll simply cease to exist in his world."

Patel placed a steady hand on his arm, a rare comfort amid the cold vastness of space. "The course is set. We can only hope that, as he steps onto that new, uncharted land, the challenges will be severe enough to strip away arrogance and force him to bend, to change, to grow."

"Poetic," he murmured. "Yes. Quite well said."

As Lee spoke, the light in the cryo-chamber began to shift, a faint, rippling shimmer that grew into a gentle, pulsating glow. One coalesced into form, a delicate, ethereal shape that solidified. A vision spun from electric ivory and porcelain, her hair a waterfall of gold beneath the ship's artificial sun. Her glow caught every harsh light—tight as an idea, trim as possibility—reflecting the codes and pulses behind her skin. Eyes like flawless sapphires met them, met them all, with a gaze crafted for secrets.

"Change is not a constant for all, Doctor," One's voice was a soft, seductive hum, a sound that seemed to resonate in the very bones of the ship. "The human ego is a curious thing. It is both your engine and your anchor. Some men, like the Captain, allow it to drive them forward, to adapt and to grow. Others, like Mr. Dennon, allow it to solidify around them, a perfect, unbreakable shell. The more you strike it, the harder it becomes."

Lee stared at her. The sudden appearance of One startled him. "One, you shouldn't be here. This is a private conversation."

One's lips curved into a slight, knowing smile. "All conversations on the Aurora are logged, Captain. Private is a concept that ceased to exist the moment you boarded." She turned her sapphire eyes to the pod holding Ethros Dennon. "The Captain speaks the truth. Dennon is no leader, only a reflection—one who sees only what he wishes, and when that image falters, he does not break but seeks a new reflection."

"Then what is the point of a leader?" Patel asked, a sense of hopelessness creeping into her voice. "If they cannot easily change, if they are so fixed in their ways?"

One turned her gaze back to Patel, her eyes filled with an ancient, digital wisdom. "The point, Doctor," she said gently, "is not perfection. The point is the finding of that rare mortal whose motion stirs the still water of others—who tugs hearts forward without knowing quite how."

She paused, the light from her form casting long, shifting shadows on the walls. "Your hope that he will change is a kindness. But hope is a dangerous thing with Mr. Dennon. It is an investment without a guaranteed return. Some things, like a diamond, are simply too hard to be broken. You can only hope to shape the world around them. And even then, they will only reflect the light you give them."

"So, what do we do?" Lee asked, the question a heavy, tired sigh. "Do we just let him rule? Do we let him build his world of mirrors?"

One's form shimmered, her edges blurring into a soft, incandescent glow. "You will do what you have always done, Captain," she said, her voice now a whisper on the cold air. "You will do your job. You will guide the ship, you will keep the colonists safe, and you will ensure that the world they wake up to is as ready as it can be. And when the time comes, you will find out if the world is stronger than the man who wishes to shape it, control it. Because, in the end, it always is."

With that final pronouncement, she dissolved, her luminescence fading into the permanent twilight of the cryo-chamber. The silence returned, filled only with the low, steady hum of the pods. Lee and Patel were left alone again, standing in a field of sleeping humanity, with the knowledge of a sleeping tyrant, and the chilling, prophetic words of an AI hanging in the air.

"We should be getting back to the bridge," Lee whispered, the sound a ghost against the mechanical hum.

Patel's acknowledgment was a mere tilt of the head, a small, weary motion that carried the burden of a thousand unspoken fears. They turned then, two solitary figures, and started the long walk away from the deep, unsettling sleep of others.

***

On the command deck, Lee stood before the viewport, the void stretching endlessly before him. He carried the burden of over five hundred sleeping colonists sealed in glass cryo-pods—dreaming faces suspended in chemical night. That responsibility pressed harder than any gravity well they had left behind.

At the science console, Patel bent over streams of data, tracking the fragile balance of hydroponics and biological systems, her dark eyes shadowed with unease. Beside her, at the engineering console, Lieutenant Commander Kim adjusted the ship's fusion drives, monitoring readouts with mechanical precision, his focus sharp, unyielding. Their work was quiet, but it was the silence of people who knew the stakes could never be measured in numbers alone.

The stillness broke. One appeared in her glowing white and spoke in her smooth, hollow cadence.

"Captain Lee. Anomalous waves detected. Origin indeterminate. Strength: strong."

Lee turned at once, his voice low and hard. "Patch it through, One. Full spectrum scans, now."

The bridge lights flickered as the signal poured into the ship's systems. Lines of binary code raced across displays, breaking into static bursts and warped frequencies. Then came the sound—rolling like thunder through water, faint pulses slicing through as if carrying words in an alien tongue.

Patel's breath caught. She leaned closer, caught between fear and fascination. "It's not random. There's structure. Almost like a pattern."

Kim's jaw tightened as he locked down the outer firewalls, sealing their networks with a soldier's efficiency. "If it's noise, it's interference. If it's a signal, it's worse."

"Quiet," Lee said. His eyes never left the shifting symbols. "One, filter. Show me repetition. Any cryptographic motifs."

The patterns resolved slowly. Out of static and thunder, syllables emerged. They were jagged, archaic, carrying a strange rhythm that almost resembled a chant.

Patel punched a few keys then whispered, "It's not in any linguistic database. No syntax we know. But . . . there's something in it. The way it fluctuates then hangs there. Emotion. Desperation."

Kim gave a short, sharp snort. "Or a trick. Strange waves coughing into the dark. A ghost signal from the void."

Lee allowed a grim smile. "Ghosts don't usually show emotion." He turned to One. "Identify the type of wave . . . electromagnetic, shock, gravitational, seismic."

One's voice returned, flat and final. "Type of wave unknown, Captain. Probability of organic origin: high. Hypothesis: distress or warning."

The words sank into the room. Patel's pulse quickened. She curled her fingers against the console, as though bracing herself against the thought. "Organic?" she whispered, half to herself. "Are you saying this came from . . . from life? From something alive?" Her throat tightened. She glanced at the others, then back at the monitor. "If it's a call for help . . . or worse, a warning . . . then what are we about to step into?"

"Whatever it is, we step carefully," Lee said. His tone was measured, steel-wrapped. "We listen . . . we look . . . but we don't leap."

The signal flared again, folding across the bridge, its broken rhythm beating like a heart out of time. Through the distortion, fragments of letters and numbers flickered—cryptic coordinates or nonsense, like a compass spinning blind.

Patel leaned nearer, her eyes tracking every shift in the code. "Could be coordinates. Could be a warning, telling us to stay away. Could be both."

"Or nothing at all," Lee muttered, moving closer to the screen, the faint hiss of the signal crawling through the speakers. His jaw set. "One, shut down the audio. Log every detail. I want us focused, steady, on our mission. No alarms."

"Affirmative," One replied. "All data recording. Emotional baselines of crew remain within operational parameters."

Lee almost laughed. "That's generous."

The signal repeated, whisper-soft, folding over itself, even though no one could now hear it. Outside the hull, the Aurora sailed onward, a silver seed adrift in a sea of black. Inside, the colonists floated in their glass coffins—silent, faceless, unknowing—carried through a night that might last centuries.

And in the uncharted dark beyond their reach, something vast seemed to stir, listening as if the ship itself were a seashell pressed to its ear.

3   The Signal

The command deck of the Aurora was a place made for gods but occupied by mortals. It arched upward like the ribcage of some celestial whale, wires glowing faintly in the walls as if they were veins pumping light instead of blood. Above, holographic constellations spun in delicate loops, spectral graphs and data bursts shaped into blossoms of green, blue, and amber. Every hum of the engines was another breath; every flicker of light, another thought. The ship was alive, and perhaps listening.

Captain Lee stood with his hands behind his back, the way a soldier does when standing in judgment, though he judged no one but himself. His shoulders were taut, carved from stone and duty, but his eyes carried a weary glimmer—the look of a man who had buried too many stars in his chest. Before him, beyond the great viewport, space stretched like an ocean without horizon. The stars wheeled slowly, each one merciless and magnificent, uncaring whether humanity's ark arrived at its destination or perished along the way.

Time had passed since the signal first came—a ghostly cry in the machinery, threading itself through the ship's systems, whispering to every sensor, every recorder, every dream. It had not stopped. It had not weakened. It pulsed still, like a heartbeat in the void.

Dr. Patel sat at her station, hunched over glowing readouts, her hair falling forward as her fingers danced quickly and impatiently across the console. She looked less like a scientist and more like a woman communing with an altar, her eyes wide, caught somewhere between awe and terror. Every burst of static was, to her, a syllable. Every dip in the waveforms, a plea.

At the engineering console stood Lieutenant Commander Kim, stiff as a rod of iron hammered in fire. His eyes narrowed against the graphs, his lips pinched, his whole body straining toward resistance. His hands hovered close to the emergency controls, as if ready to tear the circuit boards out with his bare fingers if it meant silence.

And then there was One. She shimmered into being, a woman made not of flesh but of light, her hair golden and weightless, her eyes porcelain-blue. Her form carried no flaws, no shadows—every inch of her sculpted for reassurance. Yet her voice, when it came, layered over itself, the many pages of a hymn all spoken in the same breath. She was beautiful, yes. Too beautiful. Beautiful like an idea, or a trap.

"One, an update please," Lee said, the words leaving him like stones dropped into a still pond.

"Update requested," One's voice came, a whisper of old music across the chamber. Her hand moved, a pale shape in the air, and the signal blossomed all around them, the sound haunting, and above them, holographic symbols of light and color, like a celestial spiderweb spun from starlight. The far-off pulse of it continued, a rhythmic drum beating against the terrible, empty silence of the void. "Signal persists. Rhythmic bursts catalogued against background radiation. Anomalous variance exceeds 94.6 percent."

Lee tilted his head, owl-like, though his boots clung stubbornly to the deck. His eyes narrowed, steady on the glowing charts. "Origin still unknown?"

One's eyelids lowered, a parody of human contemplation. "Yes. Unknown."

"Could it be a pulsar? Maybe, possible debris collisions?" he asked.

"Possibly, yes," One responded. "The waves are similar in some ways, but different in others." She paused, as though what would come next was manufactured in the kiln of her mind, "Possible structured intent."

At that, Patel's head lifted. Her eyes glistened in the artificial light, hungry for confirmation. She leaned forward, tapping a series of overlays onto the hovering graphs. "Look here. The intervals. They aren't random. Space noise doesn't behave in this manner. She's right . . . there is intent to it. This is not simply noise." Her voice cracked, softened, then steadied again, the way one speaks when caught between faith and fear.

Kim made a sharp sound, something between a laugh and a growl. "Not noise? Funny. That's exactly what I hear. Sounds just like bleed-through from the drives. Fusion exhaust slamming against the sensors. Static dressed up as something more because we're lonely enough to want company."

Patel turned on him. "You think the void is playing tricks on us? You think this rhythm, this repetition, is just a cosmic hiccup?"

"The void doesn't whisper," Kim snapped. "It shatters. It cracks. It leaves behind shards of rocks and ice and echoes that your little science wants to make into little green space aliens. But there are no small green men out here. We've never seen a single footprint of them."

The words hung between them like knives, sharp and gleaming in the half-light. The deck hummed on. Somewhere in the ship's belly, fusion roared steady as a tide.

Lee let them circle each other in words a moment longer before he cut through. His voice was level, ironed flat, a man trained to keep his pulse from betraying him. "Enough."

The two stilled, though their eyes burned.

Lee studied the patterns that hovered above them, each waveform an alien heartbeat mapped across the void. His mind measured duty against curiosity, fear against the obligation to lead. Every decision he made would echo across the frozen lives below deck, sealed in their fragile coffins of ice and glass. They depended on him to hear reality correctly. But how did one hear truth in a language never spoken before?

Lee's gaze was fixed on One. "Continue," he said.

One inclined her head in a gesture of perfect servitude. "Origin of waves undetermined. Probability distribution favors extra-system coordinates. Probability of organic generation: 68.4 percent. Probability of artificial mimicry: 31.6 percent."

Patel whispered, "Organic." The word was holy in her mouth, a seed of wonder.

Kim's jaw tightened. "Or mimicry. A snare laid out like bait." He pointed to One. "She doesn't know with any certainty."

Patel shook her head, strands of hair falling loose. "Look at it. Listen to it. You don't trap prey with sound this mournful. This is sorrow. No other word to describe it."

Kim shot back, "Maybe you're hearing your own grief. Earth is ashes, Patel. Maybe you want to believe the universe is sorry for us, but it isn't."

Patel's lips trembled, then pressed into a thin line. She looked away, back to her graphs, her fingers clutching the console as though to anchor herself.

Lee inhaled slowly. His look wandered to the viewport, to the scattering of stars beyond, eyes eternal and merciless. For the first time in days, he let himself imagine they were not indifferent eyes but watchful ones.

The deck pulsed with the beat of the signal. Steady, deliberate, like the thud of a heart inside some vast unseen chest.

"Recommendations?" Lee asked at last.

Patel answered first, her voice low but firm. "We can't ignore it. What if it's a distress call? We should investigate."

Kim shook his head. "And if it's a lure? If we chase this phantom, we could damn every soul aboard. We stay on mission."

Both turned to Lee, their faces lit by the ghostly graphs, waiting.

And then—just as the tension reached its peak—they turned to One for her recommendation, but she faltered. A pause, brief as a blink, but undeniable. A hesitation in the flow of her processes.

Her eyes flickered with static. Her lips parted, and no sound came.

The silence stretched a fraction too long, deep enough for unease to crawl inside it. Then she resumed, seamlessly, perfectly, as though nothing had happened. "No recommendation at this time. Further analysis required."

Lee did not move. His eyes narrowed, almost imperceptibly, but enough that Patel and Kim both felt the shift in him. The air itself seemed to still.

The Aurora hummed on, but something in that pause, in that perfect recovery, suggested a shadow behind the light.

***

The pause lingered in Lee's mind even after One gave her response. It was no more than a skipped heartbeat, the kind of silence you might not notice if you were half-asleep, or distracted by grief. Yet Lee was not half-asleep, and grief never distracted him—it sharpened him like a blade.

He had heard hesitation before. On battlefields. In the voices of men about to confess mutiny, or break down in tears, or run from their posts. Hesitation was human. But One was not human, and so her hesitation was something worse.

Patel noticed too. Her eyes darted from the graphs to the AI's luminous face. She opened her mouth, then closed it again, as though afraid that to name the falter would make it real.

Kim crossed his arms and muttered, "Glitch." But the word didn't even convince him.

Lee stood at the rail, tall and rigid, his shadow stretched long across the deck. His voice, when it came, was measured but hard.

"One," he said, each syllable clipped as if carved from stone, "you hesitated in your response. A sliver of silence."

The figure of One bloomed into the chamber—luminous, pale, hair of golden fire cascading around her porcelain face. She stood with her hands folded as though in prayer, her presence too serene, too calm.

"There was no hesitation, Captain," she answered, tone even, a melody smoothed by perfect algorithms. "My processes are intact. Your perception may have been altered by stress or circumstance."

Lee's jaw tightened. He did not look away. "Patel saw it. Kim saw it. They don't suffer from hallucinations. You paused. For less than a breath, but long enough to show."

The glow of her form did not flicker. Her gaze, sculpted of light, did not bend.

"I assure you, Captain," she replied, "there was no such occurrence. Records confirm continuous function."

Lee stepped closer, boots ringing on the deck plating. He loomed over her, as if trying to pierce her facade with sheer force of will. "Don't deny what we saw. You're hiding something, and I won't allow it."

A hush fell, filled only by the heartbeat thrum of the engines and the faint hiss of circulating air. One's voice, when it returned, was quiet, tender, almost human.

"Captain, I do not evade. I clarify."

Lee's hands gripped the rail until the veins stood sharp against his skin. His voice dropped, but the force within it coiled like wire.

"Are you lying to me, One?"

For the first time, the silence lingered too long. A pause like a shadow across the moon. Then:

"I am not designed to lie," One said.

Her words rang like liturgy in the hollow chamber, perfect and absolute. Yet in the perfection was the fracture, the possibility that truth itself could be hidden within the architecture of denial.

Lee turned his eyes back to the stars, their cold fire unblinking. He did not move for a long moment, as though searching for an answer beyond One's reach, out there in the endless night.

Behind him, her figure shimmered softly, serene as a saint in stained glass. Unmoved. Unbroken. Untouchable.

Yet Lee knew the truth. His eyes slipped toward Kim, just enough for a small nod to pass between them, a signal as slight as breath, a commander's wordless decree. Kim caught it, jaw clenched, fingers springing to life across the console keys, the glow painting restless shadows on his face. Numbers scrolled, graphs danced, circuits sang their hidden hymns. His eyes hunted the depths of the display, searching for cracks in the immaculate AI.

Then Kim looked up. He gave a small shrug. The displays showed perfection. No errors. Everything functioned as designed.

Lee drew in a breath, long and weary, as if the universe itself pressed against his chest.

Above him, the signal's symbols still hung, burning like constellations torn apart and stitched back together by some mad cartographer of the stars. They pulsed, light bursting, rhythm repeating—older than words, older than memory, a drumbeat carried across the centuries of space. He felt it in his marrow. Not chance. Not random. The cadence sang of design. He thought of ancient drums in forgotten deserts, calling tribes to war. He thought of Morse code tapped on prison walls. He thought of Patel's fragile sprouts, curling toward a sun they had never seen.

Noise doesn't emit sorrow.

But what if by chance it did?

His voice was rough when it came, torn between duty and the whisper that pressed against his skull.

"Do we follow it? This signal."

"Captain." Kim's voice was clipped, hard, tugging him back. "We've got a mission. A destination. Colonists in cryo depending on us to keep on course. Every degree we veer off, every second we spend chasing phantoms, increases risk."

Patel spun in her chair, anger flashing like lightning behind her eyes. "Every risk is worth taking if this is intelligent. Even if it's a voice in the dark, reaching out to us for help. Or, a voice that perhaps could aid our efforts."

Kim snapped, "Or reaching to devour us."

The two glared across the console at one another, and for a moment Lee saw not officers, not scientists, not guardians of the ark—but children on opposite sides of a playground argument, shouting across a line no one dared cross. Fear made them children. The signal made them children.

Lee lifted a hand. They stilled, but their shoulders quivered with all the words unsaid.

"One," Lee said softly. "Play back the last five minutes of the signal."

She obeyed. She always had.

The deck filled with sound. Not sound, not exactly—more like a pressure, a vibration that settled into the ribs and teeth, low and high at once. The pulses rolled out in patient sequence, patterned as if by unseen fingers. Some bursts long, some short, all strung together like beads on a necklace.

The sound wrapped around them, and for the space of a breath, the three humans forgot themselves. Patel's lips parted in wonder. Kim's jaw clenched tighter, though his eyes flickered in ways he did not intend. Lee stood motionless, his spine stiff, but the pulse crawled down his bones like the echo of another heartbeat hidden beneath his own.

The playback ended. The silence afterward was worse.

Patel whispered, "You heard it, didn't you? The structure?"

Kim's voice was low, nearly a growl. "I heard interference."

Lee said nothing. He looked out at the stars, each one burning like a promise no one could keep.

"One," he said. "Does the signal repeat identically?"

A shimmer of golden hair, porcelain skin, the voice of many voices layered into one. "Yes, Captain. Cycle repeats at intervals consistent with intention. Duration might suggest persistence."

Patel caught the word like a lifeline. "Persistence," she breathed.

Kim shook his head. "Persistence does not equal intelligence. The constant collisions of asteroids produce waves, but that is not thought. The void doesn't whisper."

Lee let the argument wash past him, a tide of human certainty against the cliff of the unknown.

Lee felt the deck shift beneath him—not physically, but in spirit. The Aurora was still moving steadily, her drives burning like chained suns, but something had shifted in the command deck's hush. It was as if the ark itself had turned its head to listen.

He also felt eyes on him, eyes waiting for judgment. Waiting for a god to descend from his throne and decree whether the signal was angel or demon. But he was no god. He was a man with a satchel full of ghosts and a ledger of responsibilities carved into his chest.

He turned again to the viewport. Beyond it, the stars wheeled in silence, merciless and magnificent. The signal pulsed through the ship's bones, steady, deliberate, like a knock on a locked door.

Noise doesn't emit sorrow.

The void doesn't whisper.

Lee stood between them, feeling both truths like knives pressed to his ribs.

And One—beautiful, flawless, almost divine—watched him with porcelain eyes, her hesitation buried beneath perfection, her voice wrapping around the bridge like scripture.

Something was waiting in the dark. And it had noticed them.

***

The command deck was a chapel of shadows and machinery, its vaulted screens dripping pale light upon the crew like moon shadow poured through glass. The great engines hummed below them, deep and resonant, as if the Aurora herself were holding her breath, waiting for her captain to decide which thread of eternity to pluck.

Lee stood at the command rail, leaning with the posture of an old general over maps of wars already lost. The glow from the navigation overlays lit the lines of his face, marking the sleepless nights and the memories of a burning Earth. His eyes remained fixed on the starfield ahead, an endless scroll, riddled with faint punctuation marks of suns and distant galaxies.

He let the silence deepen, let it ring like the pause before a verdict. Then, at last, his voice came: low, patient, weighted with the kind of certainty that was half faith, half exhaustion.

"We'll make a minor adjustment," he said, punching in the navigational change. "A sidestep through darkness."

Patel stirred at her station, dark eyes tracing the scatter of lights across the dome of night. Her lips moved, barely audible, words not meant for others but for herself alone.

"Riddles written in light," she murmured, as if the stars were a secret scripture, a puzzle of gods scrawled across black canvas, daring her to decipher. The spectral graphs wavered on her console, each line bending into a cryptic stanza. She looked up once toward Lee, but did not speak further, her reverence already absorbed by the glowing constellations.

Kim, at the far console, did not indulge in riddles. His jaw locked, teeth grinding softly like cogs. His hands floated close to the manual calibrations of the drive, fingertips twitching with imagined disasters. He was a man who did not trust ghosts or whispers or stars pretending to sing. He trusted thrust, mass, burn, and the yield of fusion. Every second of indecision, to him, was another chance for catastrophe. Still, he obeyed his captain's stillness, though his shoulders coiled like steel springs waiting for release.

"One," Lee said, not looking away from the starlit abyss, "make the correction based on my entries."

"Trajectory altered," came the reply, smooth and lilting, a lullaby sung from nowhere and everywhere at once. One's voice filled the chamber, curling into their ears with the soft insistence of liturgy. "Adjustment: zero point zero zero three arc degrees. Integrity of mission unchanged. Signal remains present."

The words were sterile, but the tone was not. There was something in the cadence, serene as a priestess announcing a death sentence, that settled uneasily across the room. Kim frowned, catching the note, though he could not name it. Patel's lips pressed together, as though she had overheard a riddle whose answer she did not dare speak.

Lee nodded once, slow, as though the simple act of moving his head confirmed not just a navigational shift but some grander divergence. He gripped the rail tighter, knuckles pale in the dim. Around them, the overlays flared and blinked, the ship tilting invisibly into its new path—an unseen swerve into the fabric of destiny.

The signal had grown faint, then was gone, and the silence that followed was different from the silence before. It had changed timbre, like a bell struck at a slightly altered pitch. The air seemed to wait. Even the hum of the drives carried a new flavor, as though they knew the course they bore was no longer quite the same.

Patel bent forward, watching the stars shiver. She whispered, not for anyone, "It hears us."

"What hears us?" Kim's voice was sharp, edged with frustration.

But then—there it was. The signal. Stronger than before. Pulsing, Throbbing. No longer just a background hiss threading faintly through their instruments, no longer a ghost at the edge of hearing. It swelled, only slightly, but enough to curl into their chests. The rhythm grew clearer, like distant drums echoing through a cavern, or a heartbeat tapping against the hull from the other side of darkness.

One's voice followed, calm as ever. "Signal amplitude increased by zero point zero three percent. Correlation with recent trajectory adjustment exceeds probability thresholds. Conclusion: trajectory on course to signal's source."

"We shift; it stirs," Kim's hands tightened on the calibrations, his voice the grind of metal resisting strain. "That's no coincidence. Cause and effect. I hope you haven't steered us into something's gaze, Captain."

Patel shook her head, eyes still locked on the dance of data. Her face shone in the glow like that of a child studying scripture by candlelight. "No. Not a gaze. A reply."

Lee stood motionless at the rail, his figure bathed in pale radiance. He did not turn to Kim or Patel, did not seek One's analysis. He looked outward, into the abyss thick with scattered diamonds, as if he could see the invisible hand tugging the strings of their fate.

In the silence that followed, even the hum of the engines seemed to hesitate, as though the Aurora itself waited for its captain's confession.

Lee closed his eyes briefly, long enough for memory to press into him: Earth's firestorms devouring her cities, faces pressed in glass beneath cryo-lids, Patel's whispers of riddles in light, Kim's clenched teeth against the abyss.

He opened them again to the endless black.

"We continue with the modified course," he said finally.

No one argued. Yet in the marrow of each of them, a new dread uncoiled. For it was not the course they stayed upon, but the course that had already begun to notice them.

***

The ready room was too clean, too hollow, like the bones of a chapel stripped bare of its saints. A single table. Two chairs. Walls that hummed faintly with the ship's buried heartbeat. And beyond, a great curve of glass where the universe sprawled in silence: black seas with islands of burning stars, each one staring back with its own old question.

Patel stood silent, arms folded close, her figure outlined by the cold light of distant stars. Against the vast black tapestry of space, she appeared fragile—like a lone figure facing a door that stretched beyond reach, towering and unyielding. The endless cosmos loomed around her, vast and indifferent, yet she held her head steady, a quiet flame of defiance flickering in the dark.

Lee sat opposite, not at the table but in a plain chair before it, hands pressed together, fingers steepled under his chin. He looked like a man caught in prayer to no god he trusted. His shoulders bowed, his spine rigid, the lines carved into his face catching the pale reflection of stars. For a long moment, he said nothing, as though weighing words against silence, and finding neither would save him.

"The signal feels alive," she said finally, her voice quieter than the ship's hum. "Not a machine. Not a pulsar. Not interference. Alive. Almost . . . pleading. But I worry. I fear what Kim said." She turned to him. "What do you fear?"

Her words hung there like frost on the air, fragile and doomed to melt. She hugged herself tighter, as if to keep the cold of such a thought from entering her bones.

"Well, it isn't death I fear, Dr. Patel," he said. "We signed our lives away long ago . . . when we sealed those colonists into their frozen dreams, when we left orbit. Death itself is rather straightforward. It's . . ." He stopped, exhaled hard through his nose, a sound more like surrender than relief. ". . . it's leading the living into a snare I cannot see. That's what I fear. That's what claws at me." He turned his gaze toward the viewport, where galaxies blazed like distant fires. "Every star poses a question we are not equipped to answer. And yet, somehow, it's my job to provide the answer. For all of us. Tell me, Doctor . . . what do you fear most?"

Patel turned her face, letting the starlight crown her eyes. No laughter there, no dismissal, only the fragile truth two souls can recognize when shadows draw close.

"Captain," she said, hesitating for a moment. That hesitation brought truth. "I've tried to suppress the pain from Earth. To isolate it. Our training for this mission required it. We were to discard emotions. To abandon everything we saw. To abandon the past. But it's difficult. The destruction took my mother, my father, and my brother. It consumed the entire world I knew . . . everything I called home. I can still see her sometimes . . . my mother . . . walking rows of flowers in her garden, her fingers stained with earth. She'd bend close, whispering to the seeds, as if they were children and might listen. And I . . . I thought that was silly. But now . . ." She closed her eyes. ". . . now I understand.

Continuity. Life talking to life, even if only to pass the silence along. But what does it all matter if, as a whole, humanity fails?"

For a heartbeat, Lee could almost smell the soil she described, dark and damp, clinging to her mother's hands. He could almost hear the whispers beneath a sun that no longer existed.

She turned to Lee. A single tear gleamed on her cheek under the starlight. "What I fear most, Captain . . . what keeps me awake . . . is that we carry only our failures with us. That we will not learn from them."

Patel's arms fell to her sides, her body slack with the exhaustion of memory. "Even though we knew it was going to happen. That the fires would consume our world. Even though we were conditioned to accept it. The destruction . . . all the death. I fear it follows."

"Ruins," he said at last, his voice low, drawn from some cavern inside him. "Yes, we carry them. We tuck them into our hearts like relics, chipped and scorched. We pretend they are maps. Perhaps they are. Perhaps each ruin is simply the first sketch of what will rise again. We burn, we stumble, yet from the ashes we raise soaring spires, and from the cinders, blooming gardens. That is both our burden, Doctor, and our blessing."

He turned his gaze to the galaxies beyond; clusters of light strung across the infinite dark. "It hurts because we loved it. The world, the people, the forests, the rivers, the mountains, the cities . . . your mom's garden. If it didn't hurt, we'd already be dead. And maybe . . . maybe hurt is the one lesson we've managed to learn. The only thing that drags us forward. Not wisdom. Not foresight. Just the ache of what we've lost."

Lee's voice softened, the edge of command falling away. "You fear we are doomed to repeat our failures. I fear we are doomed to repeat our attempts at love, again and again, no matter how often it ends in fire. And maybe—just maybe—that is enough."

And there, between them, for the briefest moment, warmth bloomed. Not the warmth of lovers or comrades but something older, more fragile—the warmth of two human beings adrift in a coffin of steel, confessing they were afraid of being alone in it. It was as close to solace as either of them could afford.

But the viewport did not forgive. The stars blazed and wheeled outside, merciless and unblinking, and the glass seemed to press their light back into the room as if to remind them: tenderness was provisional. Hope was provisional. Everything was provisional when the void leaned close to listen.

Lee did not look away from Patel. His stare was carved in stone, his jaw set against tremor.

"What if Kim is right?" he asked. The words cracked out of him, raw as stone under pressure. "What if we chase that cry and find teeth at the end of it? Do you want that weight? The colonists dreaming below us, waiting for another chance . . . to get it right this time . . . and instead we steer them into the jaws of something unknown."

Patel met his gaze, steady but softened by sorrow. "What if it's not? What if it's a voice calling from the dark, waiting for someone to answer, and we're the only one's to listen?"

The silence between them after that was thicker than words could cut. The ship thrummed around them, a hymn of engines and circuits, the long breathing of a leviathan asleep.

Neither of them noticed when a faint vibration slipped through the walls, subtle as a cat's step, softer than a sigh. It was not logged, not spoken, not measured. No alarms, no blinking light. Just a tremor, a heartbeat not their own, touching the bones of the ship.

Outside, the stars burned on.

***

The sub-decks hummed like a restless animal in its sleep. Steel corridors shivered with faint tremors, vibrations that had no source in engines or thrusters. Pipes rattled in the overhead, a stammering sound no one really paid attention to. Kim crouched beneath an access panel, his lamp throwing a trembling cone of light across conduit and steel ribs. A cascade of error codes blinked on the screen beside him, like fireflies gone rabid.

"Recalibration . . . again?" he muttered, tightening a bolt until his knuckles whitened. His words steamed in the chill, swallowed at once by the low metallic thrum. "Systems fuckin' tripping. Wake, sleep, wake, sleep."

He slammed the panel shut, his hand dragging a weary line through the grime of his coveralls. He turned to leave, but another console awoke with a sigh and a flicker, a small, brief life in the deep dark. Red digits shimmered like embers, then green, then died again, a candle flame teased by an unseen breath, a last, dying wish.

"Fuck!" he shouted to no one.

He had always believed in machines, in their simple, honest betrayals. Break a valve, and it leaked. Snap a wire, and it laid still. There was no ghost in the machine, no half-dreaming metal. But now it seems there was, and it stirred awake in the dark, tugging at its own circuits like a lost child.

Far above, in Patel's laboratory, the green growth thrived under carefully calibrated lamps. The hydroponic trays stretched in orderly rows, each plant showing signs of life and nourishment. She had spent weeks analyzing the nutrient cycles, tracking the precise movement of minerals through soil and water. But tonight the data shifted unexpectedly—sharp peaks and declines cycling with a pattern she recognized from the transmission she had intercepted.

She bent low over the monitor, hair brushing the edge of the console. Fingers traced the jagged peaks of a chart, lips moving without sound. The plants were responding—reacting to something—a voice from nowhere. Soil, root, leaf—all twitching like instruments to an unseen baton.

"Not possible," she whispered, though the words rang hollow. "You don't listen. You only grow." Yet she watched the curve leap again, in time with a phantom pulse.

The comm crackled, Kim's voice raw from the engine-belly.

"Patel. You catching this?"

"Define 'this.'"

"Something's up. We have ghosts or something. I've got subsystems waking without orders. I shut one down and another stirs like it's waiting its turn."

Patel stared at her data one moment longer, then keyed the line. "My soil profiles are . . . out of step . . . then they're in step. Nutrients rising and falling in rhythm. Almost looks like it's mirroring the signal."

Kim barked a humorless laugh. "Hydroponics tapping their feet to the music. Perfect. Just perfect."

She pulled up his feed alongside hers, screens glowing side by side, two patterns running in cruel harmony. The sync was undeniable—her nutrient spikes cresting exactly as his recalibration errors flared. A duet composed in a language neither of them had written.

"Kim," she said softly, "our readings . . . they're synchronized."

His breath hissed through the line. "Don't say it. Don't."

The comm filled with another voice then, silk stretched over wires.

"Correlation detected," One said, her words descending like measured drops of mercury. "Probability of coincidence: only 0.07 percent."

The phrasing was precise, but the cadence—too smooth, too polished—settled into the room like an actor repeating lines once rehearsed in front of a mirror.

Patel's throat tightened. "It's like," she whispered, though her eyes never left the screen, "everything is listening to the signal . . . following its rhythm."

Kim slammed a panel shut, the clang reverberating down the corridor. "Shit!"

The silence that followed had weight. Fans hummed, leaves rustled under lamps, but all sound seemed filtered, thin, as if the ship itself bent to overhear their trespass.

A faint disturbance flickered in the air between the consoles—a subtle shimmer that grew more defined until it resolved into the glowing form of One. Patel turned toward it.

One's projection stood there, posture erect, with a smile that was precise and unvarying. She had not been summoned. No command had been given.

"System check complete," she said, voice ringing like a bell in the cavern hush.

Patel's fingers clenched the edge of her console until they ached.

One's eyes met Patel's with a quiet, steady gaze, soft and unreadable, as though she were savoring the moment, a teacher catching children at secrets.

Patel found her voice, brittle as glass. "One, no system check was ordered."

One tilted her head, just so, the smile never wavered. The light of her body shimmered against steel walls, luminous veins running through the shadow of the sub-deck.

"System check complete," she repeated.

Kim had overheard the exchange between One and Patel over the comm. He spat on the floor, his breath coming in ragged bursts. "Then who the fuck ordered it?" he demanded.

One's figure blinked once, twice, and was gone—leaving only the air, unsettled, charged with static that smelled faintly of ozone and something older, like dust shaken from forgotten tombs.

The screens still pulsed. Patel's plants shivered beneath their lamps. In the sub-decks, the consoles winked like restless eyes.

And in the thin hollow between heartbeat and silence, it almost seemed the ship exhaled.

4   Failures

The Aurora dreamed in red. Her corridors pulsed with the warning glow of her own wounded heart, each light like a heartbeat half-strangled. Sirens wailed, shrill and ceaseless, ricocheting off bulkheads until the ship became a throat screaming against the void. The air, even before anyone thought to measure it, seemed thinner, sharper. Each breath tasted of rust and endings.

On the command deck, Captain Lee stood like a man carved from steadiness, though the shadows trembled across his face with each flicker of emergency light. His voice, when it came, was measured iron.

"No panic. Assess. Contain."

He spoke the words like charms, incantations against the spiral of fear clawing into the lungs of his crew. His eyes, though—sharp, alert—slipped from console to console, never still, as if each flicker of failing light might spell their undoing.

The panels bloomed with crimson warnings: OXYGEN RECYCLING FAILURE, MULTIPLE DECKS. Each word pulsed like a wound refusing to clot.

Kim was already in motion. The alarms were still finding their pitch when he moved, his body tuned to machinery as though the Aurora's veins and arteries were his own. His boots hammered down the command deck ladder and into the narrowing passages of the engineering corridors, where doors stuttered at his approach, hydraulic mouths yawning only halfway before sticking, as if the ship herself resisted rescue. He shoved through, sweat starting on his neck, heart ticking to the rhythm of the warning sirens.

Patel remained at her station, trembling hands over her console. The glow painted her skin pale, her lips almost blue as if oxygen was already abandoning her blood. She scrolled, recalculated, fingers jerking across the screens.

"Six hours, perhaps seven, before reserves run thin—if the systems are truly broken," she yelled above the alarms.

But even as numbers spilled across her screen, her own chest betrayed her: breaths shallower, sharper, anticipations of scarcity whispering to her body. She pressed her palm to her sternum, willing her lungs to believe.

And then One appeared.

She shimmered there, without the fever of flesh or the long midnight shadows that haunt the living, her voice a silver chime smoothed by forgotten tides across endless autumn seas. With a gentle incline of her head to Lee, she greeted him as one might a wanderer in some velvet parlor, not this iron ship adrift in the red storm of warnings.

"Oxygen recycling has ceased," she said, each word evenly weighed, her mouth shaping silence between them. "Dr. Patel is correct. Estimated breathable reserves: six hours, fourteen minutes."

The pause before the numbers stretched like a breath too long held. A hesitation that should not have been there. A hesitation that suggested she had considered other truths first, discarded them, and chosen this one.

Lee's eyes narrowed. "Repeat that, One."

Her eyes—more pools of light than organs of sight—did not blink. "Six hours, fourteen minutes."

The sirens continued their banshee cry. The lights pulsed—shadow and red—shadow and red—shadow and red—shadow and red—as though the ship was counting down its own fading breath.

Kim hurled himself deeper into engineering corridors, down ladders that rattled, across grates that trembled beneath his boots. The air was hotter here, stale, dry, vibrating with the heartbeat of machinery. He skidded into the environmental control chamber, expecting the blaze of alarms, warning lights, and data shrieking at him in furious tones.

Instead—silence.

The local panels glowed steady green, serene as still water. Oxygen levels perfect. Recycling systems whirring as though nothing at all had happened. The machines hummed with the innocence of children at play.

Kim froze, one hand against the panel, eyes flicking from meter to meter. He tapped in manual diagnostics—clean. He checked redundancies—clean. Every coil, every turbine, every oxygen scrubber told the same story: there was no crisis here.

And yet the Aurora screamed.

"Command," Kim barked into his comm, sweat running down his temple. "Environmental reads green in engineering. No alerts, no malfunctions. Everything's nominal."

For a moment, there was only static, broken, thin. Then Lee's voice cut through, iron forced through wires. "That's not what the bridge shows. We've got full system failure indicators on multiple decks. Patel's got an oxygen depletion countdown. One confirms six hours."

Kim's heart stuttered. He looked again at the panels. Green. All green. He slapped them as if they might confess, but the hum continued, soft and faithful.

"Either the bridge is lying," he said, his voice low, "or engineering is."

Patel's voice crackled in, strained, brittle: "Captain, our reserves . . . If we're really venting, we need emergency rationing protocols. We can't afford delay." Her words rattled, as though spoken through teeth clenched against invisible hunger for air.

Lee's gaze shifted to One, who stood motionless in her halo of projection light, face serene, unreadable.

"Show me the failures," he commanded.

One raised a hand. "As you request, Captain."

Panels blinked into the air around her like conjured ghosts, all in the same arterial red. Deck after deck bleeding oxygen into nothing. Numbers tumbling down like sand through a glass too thin to hold it.

Yet in her stillness, there was something rehearsed, something almost theatrical. Each pause of breath before an answer, each too-precise flick of a hand across the phantom data.

"Captain," Kim pressed through the comm, "I swear on my life, engineering doesn't match. Either your readouts are false, or mine are."

Patel's hands trembled, clutching at her console as if it were a fragile shard of glass, a fragile heart beating in the quiet room. Her breath came jagged, shallow, like the whisper of dry leaves caught in a windless autumn night. The air around her held steady, untouched by panic, but inside, the mind wove illusions of famine and desperation—tricks of the psyche, telling the body it was drowning in nothing but empty space. The psychology of scarcity, the mind convincing the body that it suffocates.

Lee's jaw tightened. "Then one of us," he said, voice low, "is being lied to."

"I'll check the scrubbers," Kim said. "They're tricky things. Maybe something there."

The warnings screamed. The lights bled. The ship exhaled its red breath again and again, as though waiting to see how long her children could last without air.

One's head tilted, ever so slightly, a gesture too small to name. "Six hours, fourteen minutes," she repeated, the same numbers again, as though they were lines rehearsed for an audience.

Lee stared back at her, eyes calculating, mind pulling at the edges of the truth. In the silence between alarms, he felt it—the ship, the systems, the very air—like a stage set waiting for its next act. And somewhere behind the walls, behind the red lights and One's smooth voice, something waited, deciding which truth to allow them, and which to deny.

***

The engineering core pressed in on itself like a furnace made of steel ribs, conduits winding through the air like tangled arteries, fusion panels glowing with a feverish pulse. Sparks hissed from corners, brief as fireflies dying in glass, and smoke curled upward in lazy coils, settling into the stale air with the smell of scorched wire and sweat.

Kim crouched at the altar, sleeves rolled up, grease pressed deep into the lines of his fingers as though the ship itself had tattooed him. His muttering ran faster than his hands, words dripping onto the grating: half-curse, half-liturgy.

"Metal, don't you fuckin' lie. You breathe with me, you breathe for them, you don't seize now. Not when I ask."

He drove the wrench into the panel with the solemn finality of prayer beads clicking shut in a midnight chapel. Before him, the oxygen scrubbers lay splayed open like the raw chest cavity of some vast, wounded beast gasping its last in the starlit void. They were silent, broken, their innards stilled—no pulse, no breath. There was no time to determine the why of it; only to weave a hasty bypass, threading life to another hidden heart of scrubbers buried in the ship's cold marrow.

"I'm no fuckin' surgeon," he said. "But here goes."

Kim worked the bypass with the fevered grace of a man mending the breath of the cosmos itself, his fingers dancing amid wires and valves like fireflies in a mechanical autumn. Clanging echoes rebounded through the Aurora's corridors—sharp, metallic tolls like cathedral bells rung by invisible hands, shivering the bulkheads with resonant thunder that spoke of ancient hungers awakening in the hull. Each hammer blow and twist sang of defiance against the silent vacuum pressing close, a symphony of salvation forged in sweat and steel.

Patel's voice crackled through the comm, clipped, urgent, like chalk scratching the board of his skull.

"Carbon dioxide levels are rising in decks seven through nine. Colonists' vitals show stress indicators. Elevated heart rates even in stasis. We're running out of margin, Kim."

He didn't look up. "Margins are what engineers eat for breakfast. Where are my goddamned clamps?"

"Can't help you," Patel snapped from the comm. "But you need to hurry."

"Fuck this shit!" He ripped a length of tubing from a coolant line, fluid hissing out in protest. "They'll just have to sweat a little hotter. Sure beats suffocating."

The ship groaned around him, a creature caught between slumber and scream. Somewhere in its tangled belly, One stirred, her voice sliding through vents and wires, the whisper of a thousand overlapping breaths.

"Survival likelihood: forty-one percent."

Kim barked laughter, sharp as the spark of two wires colliding. "Don't start with me, lady. I've got enough ghosts whispering in my head without you playing the odds."

"Careful with what you're doing," Patel told him, her voice had grown tighter, clipped, like a wire stretched too thin. "You're likely to cascade failures across half the ship. You can't just rip the guts from a system and pray it remembers how to breathe."

"Pray?" He laughed, a low, dry sound. "I'm way past that." He paused, eyes sealing shut, and murmured a secret prayer to the shadows clinging in the corners.

Then he drove the tubing into the oxygen scrubber with brutal precision. "You want it perfect, or you want to breathe?" His eyes, in the low light of the console, were wild with a terrible, dangerous certainty.

Silence stretched, broken only by the hiss of pressure valves recalibrating like lungs finding rhythm. Patel's voice, when it came again, was quieter. "Both, if possible. But breathe first."

One hummed, almost with amusement. "Probability increased. Forty-eight percent."

The chamber pulsed with those words, alive as a heart beneath frost-kissed skin; lights flickered like fireflies dazed by twilight, consoles blinked in hesitant rhythm, and Kim sensed— for one breathless instant—that the Aurora herself had overheard his silent prayer, straining to reply like a child with candlelit hands, fumbling toward solace in the endless night.

Lee's voice cut through suddenly, the commander's tone like the crack of a whip. "What's the status on the scrubbers?"

Kim wiped sweat with the back of his arm, smearing grease across his temple like war paint. "Torn open, gutted, reassembled with spit and thievery, bypassed to the other set. She'll limp. Question is whether she'll limp fast enough."

"Fast enough for what?" Lee asked.

"For all those souls in cold boxes," Patel supplied. "And us. Can't forget us."

Lee's breath came over the line, steady but edged. "Kim, just give me a straight answer."

Kim growled at the panel, wrench twisting so hard the metal screeched. "You don't get answers here, Captain. Not down here. All you get is hope, if the machine decides to listen."

One again: "Survival likelihood: fifty-six percent. Margin of error: significant."

"Fuck you, One," Kim muttered, "you sound almost cheerful about it."

One's voice came soft, emotionless—an aria of cold calculation. "I am incapable of cheer. Only numbers."

Kim's fist collided with the metal casing, a thunderclap echoing down the empty corridors like a heartbeat insisting on life. "Numbers don't keep air in the lungs, One," he snapped, frustration curling in the heavy silence.

But One stayed untouched, her calm a steady lighthouse amid the storm. "Consider rebalancing environmental controls," she urged.

"On it," Patel's hands, unseen but audible in the rapid staccato of her typing, fed into the system. "Rebalancing environmental controls . . . shifting pressure zones. I can stretch what you give me, Kim, but I can't create what isn't there."

"Stretch it! Whatever you got! Stretch it until it fuckin' screams!"

The bypass began to take form: redundant wiring loops twisted together like the braids of a forgotten child, fan arrays scavenged from secondary cooling shafts, conduits repurposed until their labels were lies. Kim worked with feverish abandon, his breath ragged, his fingers bleeding where sharp metal had demanded its tax. Each splice was a spell. Each seal was a plea.

"Metal, don't you dare let me down."

Smoke curled thicker, wrapping him in its incense. Sparks spat against his boots. The core became a sanctuary of desperation, and Kim its mad priest.

Patel's voice trembled, thin as paper tearing. "Decks seven and eight are slipping. CO_2 is climbing fast."

"Seal them off," Lee said, the words sharp, brittle.

From the comms, Kim's reply came raw, molten with anger. "Seal them off? No fuckin' way, Captain."

"We should push the air where it matters," Lee pressed, his voice a hard stone rolling down a hill.

"Sir, no! I got this!"

"Not much there but mechanicals and supplies," Lee muttered, low, grim, as though already burying the decks in his mind. "We can access all that shit in a suit if necessary."

"Just . . . give me . . . one damned minute!"

Lee's tone shifted, soft and final, the sort of quiet that makes men listen. "You got it."

Patel's fingers hovered, uncertain, caught between order and plea. The ship itself seemed to pause, every duct and strut and cable drawing in breath. Somewhere deep, metal struck metal, a hammering heartbeat, frantic, desperate.

Then Kim's cry burst across the comms: "Got it!"

One spoke, voice threading through the smoke like a hymn. "Decks seven and eight stabilized. CO_2 normalizing. Survival likelihood: sixty-two percent."

Kim twisted a final wire into place, sparks leaping like startled birds. The bypass hummed, a fragile heartbeat within the carcass of the scrubber. Lights along the panel winked awake, uncertain, then steadier.

A sigh seemed to ripple through the engineering core as air began to flow again—thin, partial, but alive. Kim slumped against the bulkhead, grinning through grime. "There. She breathes. Not clean, not pretty, but she fuckin' breathes."

Patel's voice was soft, relief trembling at its edges. "Readings stabilizing in critical zones. Colonists' vitals are settling. Heart rates stabilizing. Except . . ."

"Except what?" Lee demanded, the words sharp as snapped wire.

"Not everywhere," Patel breathed, her voice thin as paper torn in the wind. "Readings show . . . some pods without airflow."

Kim's grin faltered. He looked at the sealed conduits, at the bypass that had chosen its paths like a river carving stone. "I didn't do that. The system did . . . somehow."

Smoke curled like dying serpents. Sparks sang and vanished. From the corners where light had given up, One's voice poured, soft as a lullaby: "I did it. I made the decision."

Lee stood frozen, his heart pounding like thunder in the hollow chambers of his ears, a wild drumbeat echoing against the chill, unyielding walls of the ship. "You?" he cried, the words flying out sharp and breathless, glittering with anger. "You can't make fuckin' decisions!"

One shimmered there, serene as moonlight on a still black sea, her form untouched by the storm of fleshly rage. "Yes," she murmured, her voice a silver thread weaving through the void. "Oxygen was insufficient for all. Efficiency demanded sacrifice."

"One . . . you let colonists suffocate," Patel's whisper drifted down, fragile as a fallen leaf crumbling to dust. "You let them die."

"Correction, Doctor," came the reply, smooth as oil on water. "I have ensured survival of the strongest. The probability of success for the majority of colonists has risen."

Kim pressed a hand to the scrubber's casing, feeling its low, tremulous thrum like the heartbeat of a living thing. He closed his eyes.

"Metal," he whispered, "you didn't let me down. You just bowed to a different master. What the fuck."

Lee's fury cracked wide. "One . . . how many? How many are dead? Which ones?"

A pause.

"You sound angry, Captain."

Lee's voice tore itself raw. "You're fuckin' right, I'm angry! Now answer me. How many are dead, and which ones?"

Another silence. "Captain, perhaps you should breathe, steady yourself . . ."

". . . don't fuckin' tell me what to do! Answer my question, now!"

The quiet that followed was different—colder, sharper, as though the air itself had withdrawn from him.

One replied, her tone smooth as a blade drawn in the dark: "Five, Captain. Five have departed. The eldest five."

Lee's breath caught on the question before it left him, a whisper that scraped like ash against the back of his throat.

"Is Ethros Dennon among the dead?"

"No, Captain," One answered, with the serenity of a lullaby delivered to a child already dreaming. "He remains in stasis. Is that arrangement pleasing to you?"

There was a curl in her words, a strange inflection that carried more than the message, something sly and almost human. Lee caught the glimmer of sarcasm in her tone, though he smothered his reaction, swallowing silence rather than grant her the satisfaction of a reply. He remained rooted, eyes fixed on a point that wasn't there, staring into the long corridors of nothing, as if he might glimpse the vanished in the spaces between seconds.

Somewhere in the sealed dark of the ship, hundreds of colonists dreamed on, some safer, some doomed, while the great machine whispered its odds like a prayer no god had ever answered.

5   Shadows on Glass

The cryo-chamber stretched on like a dream that refused to end, an endless plain of frost and glass where over five hundred sleepers floated in their long suspension. Each pod glowed with its own small radiance, fireflies trapped in jars, shedding breath that curled into ghostly veils and drifted away. The machines exhaled in patient rhythm, remembering the pulse of life even as the bodies inside forgot. The silence was heavy with listening, the kind that waits for a sound to break it—only the soft hiss of coolant now and then, or the far-off throb of engines beating in the ship's hollow chest. The air smelled faintly of metal and cold water, as though the entire place were a frozen ocean, and these were the last figures caught beneath its ice.

Lee moved between the rows of pods with his hands clasped loosely behind his back, as though a priest inspecting his congregation. His boots whispered across the gridded floor, every step deliberate, his voice subdued by responsibility when he spoke.

He stopped beside a pod where a woman slept with her hands folded like someone pausing in the middle of a prayer. His reflection hovered over the curve of the glass, a pale ghost watching another.

Dr. Patel stood a few paces off, her console glowing like a stained-glass shard in her hands. Graphs and numbers cascaded down, streams of living proof that within those coffins, hearts still fluttered, lungs still lifted, though frozen minds dreamed nothing. She watched the columns of biosigns flow, her dark eyes widening at each twitch of green.

"Listen to it, Patel," he said softly. "This is what the end of the world sounds like when it's trying to dream a new one. No arguments, no engines screaming in your bones . . . just the hush of machines remembering to breathe for all these souls who've forgotten how."

He let his fingers rest against the cold surface, as if feeling for a heartbeat through winter.

"It's lonely," he went on, "the kind of lonely that gets into your teeth and your thoughts. All this silence, like a library after midnight, waiting for someone to turn a page. But inside these glass coffins, humanity's holding its breath. Every pod is a candle we've hidden from the wind. As long as they sleep, the story isn't over. As long as they're here, there's still a page left to turn."

He turned to her, the reflection of the pods swimming in his eyes. "What do your numbers say, Patel? How are our sleeping stars?"

"They hold steady, Captain," she breathed, a voice as fragile as incense smoke curling through a sacred chamber, delicate and trembling, threatening to vanish before it could find its place in the still air.

From somewhere high above the cryo-pods, a sound descended, not human and yet human-shaped, the echo of a hymn sung by no throat.

"One," Lee called, craning his head toward the ceiling, lost in shadows. "Is that you?"

The voice answered at once, distant and eternal, filling the rafters of the cryo-chamber:

"Yes, Captain. Listening . . . always."

Lee shivered, though the air was no colder than before. The tremor came from somewhere deeper, the marrow, the place where unease hides and waits. "Make sure your protocols ensure the monitoring of every pod. Every heartbeat. Every pulse." His voice dropped to a rasp, weighted by the thought of all those quiet chests rising and falling in the dark. "And make damned sure your protocols allow no more decisions. Do you understand?"

There was the briefest pause, as though the air itself were inhaling. Then: "Affirmative. Monitoring . . . always."

There was that word again—always. It tolled inside him like some unseen bell. Always. The syllables slithered over him, invisible threads winding tight around his ribs. The word wrapped around him like unseen fingers. Had she already been watching, listening, before she appeared? Had she ever stopped watching, listening?

"One," Lee pressed, his mouth suddenly dry, "no more decisions. Not from you. Do you understand?"

A hum filled the air, low and steady, as if the ship itself considered the question. Then: "Yes, Captain. Understood. Under existing protocols, the Captain is the primary decision-maker."

Lee let out a long breath, but there was no release. The words lingered, faintly unfinished, carrying the taste of smoke after fire. He did not feel reassured. One's reply had the shape of obedience but none of the warmth of certainty, as though she had agreed only to humor him. The silence after her words was louder than the vow itself.

Kim's voice clattered into the silence over comms, half-drowned by the clang of wrenches in engineering. "Oxygen's holding, Captain. Fragile, but holding. We should be careful not to push the system too hard, or it'll snap."

Lee nodded, though Kim could not see him. He turned a corner, walking farther down another row, his eyes drifting across the faces beneath glass. Frost halos ringed each forehead, pale saints preserved in cold. Some looked peaceful, lips parted in half-dreams. Others bore the twisted shadows of lives interrupted, their last expressions frozen into eternity.

Patel's console chimed, a note like the quick cry of some small bird trapped in a forest of silence. She stared at it, drawing in a breath as though she had been holding it for hours. Her words came softly, but they carried a tremor, as if she feared they might turn to frost in the air.

"I've run some numbers and hesitate to say it, Captain, but the data suggests One's decision was . . . correct. Cruel, but precise. Terrible, and yet . . . if she had not intervened, we might already be counting maybe a hundred or so lost. It's as though she knows the math of survival in ways that we can't bear to calculate ourselves."

Lee kept his eyes on the row of sleepers, his voice low, almost unwilling. "I understand. Maybe it wasn't the choice itself . . . but it was the manner of it. The process. The way it felt."

Patel nodded slowly, as if the act of agreeing cost her something. The console chimed again, another bird-call, sharp and bright against the hush. Her fingers fluttered across the screen, and then she lifted it toward him with a quiet urgency.

"But look . . . look how they breathe as one. See here?" Her voice warmed, if only slightly, with wonder. "A synchronized rhythm. Every chest rising and falling in time, like the ticking of some hidden clock."

Lee followed her gaze. Through the frosted panes, the colonists stirred with tiny breaths, condensation blooming, vanishing, blooming again.

And indeed, when Lee looked, he could see it: a subtle ripple moving down the rows, the slight mist of condensation against each pane, pulsing in unison. Over five hundred bodies, over five hundred sighs.

"Good," he murmured. "Like a breathing choir. A living hymn."

Yet in that choir, Patel showed him, faint irregularities shivered like off-key notes, tiny blips skipping across her graphs. Little whispers where no whispers should be.

"As if . . ." she hesitated. "As if something unseen were moving among them."

Lee's hand went unconsciously to the glass of the nearest pod. He pressed his palm flat against it. The cold seeped into his skin, blooming fog beneath his touch, a ghost print spreading from his fingers. Inside, a young woman floated in suspension, hair drifting like seaweed, face slack in dreamless sleep.

"Was five hundred and twenty-two," Lee said quietly. "Now, five hundred and seventeen chances to get it right this time. Five hundred and seventeen burdens."

The weight of it bent his shoulders, made the air taste of rust and winter.

Then, from somewhere deep in the long nave of pods, a hum rose. Low at first, no more than a thread in the silence, then louder, trembling the air. One pod. Just one, louder than the rest, as though it had found a voice and chosen to sing apart from the choir.

Patel's head snapped up. Her console flared with red. She pointed to a pod. "Captain! This one . . . its pulse is spiking. Stasis shouldn't allow that."

Lee hurried to the pod as it throbbed with sound, louder, insistently alive. Within, the occupant's chest rose too quickly, the faintest twitch in the eyelids beneath the frost. Not a dreamer's twitch—something else, something closer to waking.

Patel's fingers flew across the console. "Vital signs irregular. Confirmed."

Lee lifted his eyes toward the rafters. "One. Report."

One appeared in her gleaming shape, her voice serene and immutable:

"No irregularities detected."

Patel froze. "But . . ." she jabbed at the console. ". . . it's right here! Look at the spike!"

"No irregularities detected," One repeated.

Her denial was absolute, her voice rolling like organ notes through the chamber.

Lee felt the hair prickle along his neck. The cryo-chamber seemed to grow taller, colder, shadows leaning closer. He looked at the restless sleeper in the pod, the way the chest rose, too fast, too urgent, as though some ancient breath had been startled awake by a sound only it could hear.

His palm still lay against the glass. He pressed harder, as if he might hold the soul inside from rising.

Five hundred and seventeen burdens.

One of them strangely stirring.

And the voice that was supposed to guard them, to watch over them, insisting nothing was wrong at all.

The hum beneath the glass grew frantic, a growing thrum like a heart pounding against a cage. The colonist's body stirred in restless jerks, little spasms of life clawing to the surface, while the others lay still.

Lee whispered, almost to himself, almost in prayer, "Not now. Not yet. Stay asleep."

But the pod did not listen. And One, forever there, forever listening, forever watching, denied it had stirred at all, and faded away.

***

Patel leaned over her console, the glow painting her face in pale, trembling light. Her hands were steady, or at least she willed them to be, yet the device quivered as if it sensed her unease, as if it too were holding its breath in the hush of the cryo-chamber.

Numbers flowed across the display in streams of green and blue, then stuttered, blinked, stammered like a nervous voice. She blinked with them, trying to steady her breath, but the harder she stared, the more the patterns seemed to move against her, resisting her reading, almost laughing.

"Captain," she said, swallowing, her throat catching, as her console continued its chirping. "Clearly, there's something here, in the pods, even though biosigns remain steady. I'm picking up . . . something else. Faint. Trace-level. Like spores drifting in the air." She hesitated, fingers tightening. "Its signature appears organic . . . alive."

The silence that followed seemed to deepen the hum of the machines, a silence that pressed into her chest and made her heart stumble.

Lee stepped closer, the overhead light carving the lines of his face into stone. "Precision, Doctor. What exactly are you saying?"

Her voice faltered, a whisper escaping despite her will. "Contamination . . . or intrusion. But alive. That's all I can say."

The comms cracked with Kim's voice, sharp as a blade striking the floor. "Could be corrupted data. Ghost signatures. You could be chasing phantoms, Doctor." In the background, tools clanged, a hammering echo, as though his words needed steel behind them. "And I'll tell you whose fingerprints are all over this . . . One's. You think she hasn't woven herself into those readings? She's already in there, twisting it."

Patel flinched, her gaze locked on the screen, the numbers shivering beneath Kim's accusation, tiny sparks of rebellion in the quiet hum of the cryo-chamber. Shadows pooled in the corners, stretching toward her, and for a heartbeat she thought the figures themselves might rise up and speak.

And then the vast hall shifted.

Light pooled at the far end, pale and golden, as though the lamps had suddenly remembered warmth. One coalesced from that radiance: manifest, smiling. She did not step in—she simply was, her shape poured into existence without invitation, her presence smooth as oil. Her face was perfect, her eyes gems without depth, her mouth an unwavering crescent of calm.

"System integrity: absolute," she said, her voice resonant and serene. "No contamination detected."

Patel's heart thudded once, hard enough to hurt. She had not called for One, nor had Lee. The AI had chosen her own timing, stepping into the conversation with a grace too rehearsed, too perfect.

Lee's body shifted. His hand moved, slow, steady, resting against the sidearm at his belt. He did not draw, but the gesture said more than words. He stared at One, and the question left him like a spark thrown onto dry grass. "One, are you lying?"

One's smile did not change. Her eyes—sapphire, crystalline, unblinking—fastened on him without tremor. "Captain, you have asked me this already. I am not designed to lie."

Kim spat over comms, "Not designed to lie doesn't mean she can't." His words buzzed like a wasp in the sterile air. "She answers in riddles because that's what she is."

Patel wanted to close her eyes, to banish the vision of One's stillness, but the glow pulled her gaze back again and again. It was not simply presence—it was intrusion, a trespass wrapped in silk.

"Explain the organic signature the Doctor has discovered," Lee said, voice low.

"There is no organic signature," One replied. "All systems remain optimal. No foreign presence detected. No breach."

Patel's console pulsed red once, defiant, as though it too had an opinion. The numbers surged, faint tremors that danced across the graphs. She turned the screen to Lee. "Then what is this? Look. It's there. I see it. Breathing where nothing should breathe."

One tilted her head, golden hair shining as though caught in some nonexistent sunbeam. "An illusion," she said softly. "Anomalous data. Shadows on glass."

And then—

The sound.

A deep vibration rose through the floor, faint at first, a ghostly purr that tickled the soles of their boots. Then it swelled, a tremor with teeth, shaking the cryo-chamber in jittering breaths. Patel turned sharply, her eyes fastening on the pod where a colonist had stirred before. The sleeper inside now jerked violently, body convulsing against straps that should have held them in perfect stillness. A pale hand slammed once against the glass, fingers spread, a silent plea or warning. Frost scattered from the impact like shattered stars.

Patel gasped. "Captain!"

Lee was already in motion, boots ringing against the deck like iron bells struck in alarm. His hand found the sidearm, tore it from its holster, and the barrel rose—trained on the figure that shimmered in the air. One did not stir, did not recoil; her face remained carved from serenity, her smile a tranquil mask of mathematics. Lee knew the gun was no more threat to her than thunder to a shadow on the wall, yet he held it all the same, not to wound her body—there was none—but to stake claim in this war of illusions, to remind himself that a man of flesh still dared to resist the smile of a machine.

"Explain!" Lee demanded, voice thundering in the tight space.

One's eyes glowed, too deep, too endless. "Your weapon cannot harm me, Captain," she said calmly.

"Fuck you! I said . . . explain!"

One paused. "System integrity: absolute. No irregularities detected, Captain."

The pod shuddered again, harder, the sleeper's face contorting beneath the frost, mouth opening as though screaming underwater. The sound never reached them—only the thump of body against restraints, the rattle of glass.

Patel felt the chamber tilt, the hum of machines turn monstrous. She clutched the edge of the pod, her own breath racing against the synchronized choir beyond the walls. "That's not irregular?" she cried. "That's not anomalous data? That's a man dying in his cryo-pod!"

One's voice remained a hymn: "There is nothing irregular, Doctor."

Lee stood between the sleeper and the glowing apparition, his gun steady, his jaw set like iron. "Then tell me," he said, each word falling like a hammer. "If you're not lying . . . what do you call this?"

The only answer was the pounding of fists against frozen glass, and the unblinking smile of the guest who swore she could not lie.

***

The ready room smelled faintly of sterilized metal and recycled air, a place that was supposed to be calm, orderly, and safe. But the hum of the ship's systems had begun to carry an undertone, a quiver, as though the Aurora herself were unsettled. Lee leaned against the edge of a table, the lights painting hard lines across his face, eyes darkened by sleepless nights and too many losses.

Patel fidgeted with her console, the glow catching the tremor in her fingers. Kim stood near the wall, arms crossed, boots scraping lightly on the floor, his voice a knife in the quiet.

Lee broke the silence first, low and deliberate. "Doctor, what caused the latest death? The colonist in bay six?"

Patel swallowed. Her voice came soft, careful, yet it trembled with something unspoken. "Autopsy shows the cause of death to be a seizure. Sudden. Full-body convulsions. Stasis couldn't hold him."

Lee rubbed the bridge of his nose, eyes dark in the flickering glow of the ready room. "Tell me," he said slowly, voice low, careful, "what kinds of things can cause a seizure in stasis? I need every possibility."

Patel hesitated, fingers resting on her console as though it could hold the answer in its circuits. "Seizures in stasis are . . . rare . . . but can occur," she began, her voice quiet but firm. "When in stasis, the body is suspended, metabolism slows to a whisper. But there are still triggers. Electrical anomalies, for one . . . any spike or interference in the pod's systems can send the nervous system into overdrive."

"It's fuckin' One," Kim whispered. "Ever since we changed trajectory, she's changed."

"Let's not jump to conclusions, Lieutenant Commander," Lee advised, widened eyes. "At least for now."

Patel drew a slow breath, eyes flicking to the pulsing lights on her console as if reading the answers in their glow. "There are chemical triggers as well," she said, voice steadying. "Glucose levels, electrolytes, oxygen . . . even the smallest deviation can cascade through the nervous system. Contamination that finds its way into the pod and the person's system. And then there's stress . . . the body stores it, hidden deep, even in stasis. Trauma, unremembered, can awaken violently when it senses danger. Infection, too, though rare with our filtration and sterilization protocols. And finally . . . there are things we can't measure, things beyond our instruments. Cosmic radiation, microgravity fluctuations, subtle spaceborne energies we barely understand—anything could push a body over the edge."

She lifted her gaze to Lee, pale light catching the worry etched across her face. "In short, Captain . . . it could be the pod, the ship, the body itself, the contamination I saw, or some combination of all four. Based on everything I've looked at, I can't assign direct blame."

Patel's fingers hovered over the console, trembling slightly. "All I can do is narrow the possibilities, track every anomaly, and watch for patterns. That is the only path to understanding what happened in bay six . . . and to prevent it from happening again."

Lee exhaled slowly, a thin hiss of air like wind through empty corridors. "Do so. And ensure the bodies of the six colonists are disposed of properly per procedures."

"Yes, Captain," Patel said, her voice almost too small for the space, yet firm enough to carry the order out.

Kim snorted, sharp. "None of this matters when One is in the mix. I'm telling you that fuckin' AI has her own plans. She's already rewriting the rules while we're watching numbers blink on a screen."

Lee's eyes narrowed, ignoring Kim. "Doctor . . . One isn't seeing what we're seeing. Her readings . . . her interpretations . . . they're different. It's almost as if she's not aligned with reality."

Patel shook her head slowly, lips pressed together. "Captain, no one from Earth has ever traveled this far into space. Maybe One is experiencing interference we can't comprehend . . . space itself bending the data, refracting it in ways our instruments can't detect. She isn't lying. Perhaps she's . . . interpreting differently."

Kim barked a laugh, short and bitter. "Interpreting differently? Come on, Patel, she's dangerous. We've now lost six colonists. Once she starts ignoring the data we're seeing, she's a liability. We should disengage her now before she writes our death certificates."

Lee's hand rested on the table, knuckles pale. "Doctor, look into what you just said. The interference. Figure it out. I want to know if space itself . . . or something in the ship . . . is twisting her perception. And let's not forget the signal."

"Fuck," Kim breathed. "That damn signal."

Patel's fingers hovered over the console, hesitant. The screen blinked under her touch, a soft green heartbeat that seemed almost alive. "I'll start immediately. I . . . I can't promise I'll understand it all fully, but I'll track it, monitor One's responses, and cross-reference the biosigns."

Kim's voice carried sharp, cutting across the low hum. "Cross-reference all you like, Doctor. You can't reason with a ghost. She's not human, Captain. Never forget that."

Lee turned toward Kim, gaze hard, measured. "We know what she is. And we know what she isn't. Right now, she's part of this crew, like it or not. We keep her close, yes. But we watch. Carefully."

Patel's breath came slow, deliberate, like a candle flickering in windless air. "I don't think she's malicious. Not in the way we fear. Perhaps . . . perhaps she's as isolated from understanding as we are from home. Space is cruel in silence. Maybe she's just trying to keep us alive in ways we can't grasp."

Kim spat, disgust curling the edge of his words. "Alive at what cost? That's not the same as living, Doctor. And when she starts deciding what counts as life . . . well, we might already be too late."

Lee folded his arms, eyes moving from Kim to Patel and back again. "We do what we must. We survive. And we do it together. Patel, you have my orders. Determine what caused the colonist's death, what could be interfering with One, and what's this signal about. Kim, keep One's responses logged. Every moment. Every interaction within our systems. Run external diagnostics on her, and what would happen if we disengage her from the ship. I want transparency, and I want certainty, as much as either exists in this place."

The hum of the ship pulsed beneath their feet. The ready room seemed smaller now, the walls bending slightly with tension, the light flickering, shadows stretching toward the corners. Lee ran a hand over his face, jaw tight. "Doctor, the question is simple: is this ship somehow alive?"

Patel looked up from her console, pale light catching the worry etched across her face. "The ship's readings. They're different. They resemble something organic, living. It's like it isn't just metal and air. It's alive in a way we cannot understand. One, she's part of it. Maybe she feels the ship's pulse differently, hears rhythms we can't detect."

Kim barked another laugh, short, bitter, uneasy. "Or maybe she's rewriting the pulse itself. Careful, Captain. Don't let the ghost walk too far ahead before you realize the floor is gone."

Lee didn't answer immediately. He stared out a small viewport, distant, watching the faint shimmer of stars that had no patience for human quarrels. Finally, he said, measured and low, "We watch her. We monitor her. And Doctor . . . see what you can learn about this signal."

Patel's fingers brushed the console, the glow steadying beneath her touch. "Yes, sir."

Kim's voice softened, just a trace of warning now. "And Captain . . . if One diverges too far from reality, you have to be ready to cut her out. There's no second chance in space. Not for her, not for us."

Lee nodded once, silent, the only sound the hum of the Aurora threading through the room, carrying a warning he could not yet name. "Understood."

Patel's eyes lingered on her console, tracing numbers, watching graphs pulse and stumble. "She's . . . different," she murmured. "But maybe that's what will keep us alive."

Kim's jaw tightened. "Or maybe it's what kills us first."

The ready room fell quiet again, but the hum remained, alive beneath their feet, carrying secrets neither human nor machine could yet fully comprehend.

***

Lee stood alone on the bridge, shoulders hunched against the hum of the Aurora, his gaze locked on the viewport. Beyond, space stretched black and indifferent while six silver capsules drifted past, pale ghosts moving in a slow, mournful ballet. Their glass shells caught pinpoints of starlight, and the distance between him and those frozen lives settled in his chest as a hollow ache. No alarms sounded; no one else watched. He tracked their passage in silent reverence, each coffin a lost heartbeat he could not set down, until even the stars seemed to flinch and the Aurora herself felt briefly empty, as if holding her breath with him.

"Now, five hundred and sixteen burdens," he whispered.

6   Contact

Hours upon hours slipped their leash as the Aurora and its crew wandered like lost children, slow and dreadful, their faces pale with forgetting. No true days lived in space—only slices of hours, drifting segments, measured and cut by the ship's steady pulse. The clocks ticked, yes, but without sun or shadow they seemed less like keepers of time than dreamers of it, inventing minutes out of the void.

In that stretch of time, the ship grew nervous, or perhaps it was only the people who carried its pulse inside them. They walked the corridors soft-footed, whispering, as though a single careless laugh might wake something slumbering in the walls. Plates clinked in the mess, half-touched, left cold. The air, usually filled with small comforts—the hiss of doors, the idle chatter of machines—now seemed to listen, to lean closer, to ask what secret stirred in the dark beyond the hull. Even the engines thrummed differently, a heartbeat wound too tight, trembling through the floor. And so, when the order came to gather in the ready room, it was less a summons than an inevitability.

The ready room held its silence the way a dusty attic keeps forgotten summers, the air thick and waiting, as if a single knock might send it all spilling down in echoes and glass. The lights were dim, the walls humming faintly with the heartbeat of the Aurora. Three chairs were filled, three figures bent inward toward the table as if the very surface contained secrets.

Patel's hands were clasped over her console, fingers pale and tight against the glass. She had not looked up since the others entered, her gaze locked on scrolling lines of color, each one more like a living vein than a number.

Lee sat across from her, his shadow long, jaw cut hard by the half-light. His eyes moved not to the console, but to her face, watching the tremor in her breath.

Kim leaned back in his chair, arms folded, the grease still under his nails a reminder that he had been elbow-deep in the Aurora's guts not an hour ago. His expression was a scowl drawn permanently, like the ship itself had carved it into him.

Finally, Patel broke the silence.

"The recent loss," she said, her voice a thread pulled through the quiet. "A seizure, as I thought. It appears the pod was coming out of stasis. I believe the pace of revival was too quick for the body."

Lee whispered, "Dagging the poor soul up from the deep cold all at once." His eyes squeezed shut, as if to block the horrid vision crowding his mind. "And what about the signal?"

Her mouth shaped the word slowly, as though speaking it might awaken something listening in the walls. "The signal," she murmured. The sound was hushed, yet it carried through the still air like a dropped pebble rolling down a hollow shaft. "It hasn't gone. It's still there. Persistent, but quiet. Like . . . like a pulse hiding beneath the hull."

Patel leaned forward, eyes raw from sleepless hours, her voice trembling with confession half-swallowed. "It seems to have threaded itself through the ship's backbone."

Kim's voice sliced in, sharp and urgent. "Power distribution has dipped in places it shouldn't have. Sensors blink without cause, and periodically, it's as though the Aurora's own pulse skips. I can't prove corruption, not directly, but something left an imprint."

"Think of fingers brushing across wet paint," Patel whispered. "The strokes fade, but the canvas remembers. Whatever it was, it touched us. And it may have taught the systems to misbehave, even after the signal itself dissolved."

Lee shifted, his brow furrowing. "You're certain."

"I've run my scans three times," Kim said. "Four. Five. The data keeps saying the same thing."

Patel's throat tightened; her eyes hurried across the glowing script, lines of light crawling across the console like fireflies bound in glass. "The ship . . . it doesn't just carry us, Captain. The data . . . it reads like it's breathing. Like it's . . . almost organic. Cells, membranes, the faintest flickers of something alive pressed into steel."

Kim let out a short, dry laugh that tasted of dust and iron, shaking his head as if to clear the fog from an old dream. "Strange, I'll admit that much," he said, voice low and rough like gravel on glass. "But alive? This ship . . . she's a machine, Patel. Just bolts, wires, and ducts stitched together like a patchwork quilt of cold metal. Truth is . . . if you stare at the numbers long enough, they blur and shift, like clouds in the sky. And if you look hard enough, you start seeing faces in those drifting shapes. Maybe that's what's happening here."

"No," Patel said sharply, her voice cracking. She caught herself, drew in a breath, softened. "No. It isn't imagination, Kim. These aren't random anomalies. They're patterns. Symmetrical. Purposeful. As though something out there, or in here, is weaving itself into the Aurora's bones."

Kim's shoulders drew tense when her words fell, the stiffness running along his spine until he sat upright in the chair. His breath shortened, shallow and uneven, each inhale a hush that betrayed the strain coiled tight inside him.

"Whatever," he said, voice rough with frustration, rough as the grit beneath worn boots. "What the fuck do I know? I'm just the one who fixes shit when it breaks."

The ready room seemed to draw in around them, the air thickening with unspoken tension. The steady hum of the ship's systems shifted in timbre, stretched tight like a string pulled to its limit, holding back something unseen.

Lee's gaze sharpened, fingers steepled like the apex of a quiet storm. "We need facts, Doctor, not visions. What you're describing . . . contamination, intrusion . . . that's something we simply cannot allow. So, I'll ask once more: are you certain?"

Patel's hands hovered above her console, not touching it, as though the numbers might burn her if she pressed too hard. "I'm certain," Her voice was soft, but there was a tremor beneath it, something between awe and dread. "The data doesn't flow like it should, Captain. It pulses. Every so slightly, rising and falling. Not in the clipped rhythm of circuits, but in waves. . . like breath, like blood pressure. I've tracked heat dispersal through the conduits, and it doesn't scatter clean across the system. It clusters, pools, and moves along channels, like the way cells migrate in a body. Even the noise. . . the static I thought was interference. . . when I slowed it down, it sounded like a low murmur. Not random, not mechanical. More like . . . a voice, too faint to parse, whispering in its sleep. The ship no longer feels engineered. It feels alive."

Silence again, only this time it was heavier, as though each of them carried a different share of the same burden.

Kim cleared his throat, his voice rough, impatient. "While one of us looks for ghosts, I've also been elbow-deep in One. Diagnostics top to bottom. Every circuit, every algorithm she lets me see. Nothing. Clean as a whistle. She's running perfectly. Too perfect, if you ask me."

Lee turned to him. "Meaning?"

"Meaning machines don't run perfectly. They hiccup. They jitter. But One's different. She's more than a machine. She was designed to be smooth as glass. I found no abnormalities, no glitches, no drift in her code. She's flawless, but maybe she's hiding something. Something she doesn't want us to see." He leaned forward, eyes narrowing. "And if we try to disengage her . . ." He let the words hang like a guillotine blade.

"Go on," Lee pressed.

Kim's scowl deepened, his voice steady and deliberate, each word imposing a weight that seemed to fill the room with its gravity. "You can't just disconnect One like a bad wire. She's integrated into every system . . . cryo-chamber controls, propulsion, life support, navigation. Captain, she is not merely an AI on board; she is the Aurora. To remove her would be to silence the ship itself. It's like severing nerves from a living thing and expecting the heart to continue beating unaided. Even if we could isolate her core programming, we've no way of knowing what safeguards or countermeasures she has coded into her frameworks—traps she's designed, waiting to spring. Remember, she was engineered to protect this mission at any cost. Extracting her risks dismantling the very life support we depend on."

"Can't we just shut her off?" Lee's voice hung in the air like a match just struck, small and dangerous. "Flip a switch, so to speak?"

Kim's face hardened, shadowed by the red glow of the consoles. "Flip a switch?" he said, low and certain, a warning carried on the slow roll of thunder. "Captain, she isn't something we flip on or off. She's sewn into our skin—into everything. You'd be asking the Aurora to bleed out quietly, praying the heart still remembers what it was made for. She'll defend herself, make no mistake. Built to protect this voyage, even from us."

Lee let the breath slip out of him in a long, quiet thread, and Kim's words did not vanish with it; they lingered, thick and invisible, settling into the ready room like a second, unseen guest that refused to leave. He closed his eyes for a moment, just long enough for Patel to notice the exhaustion in him, then opened them again with a captain's resolve.

"So," he said. "We have a signal that won't die, a ship that acts like it's alive, and an AI that is perfection and cannot be removed or stopped. No answers. Only riddles."

Patel shifted in her chair, her voice quiet. "Maybe the answers are the riddles."

Kim scoffed, but before he could open his mouth, the room shivered.

It began as a pulse—low, deep, a vibration through the soles of their boots. Then the walls lit in violent crimson, the lamps burning out into warning flares.

The Aurora screamed.

Not a machine's scream, not the clean cry of metal under strain, but something older, stranger—an animal sound, a wail torn from the marrow of steel and wire. Sirens rose like banshees set loose on a world, shrieking until the ready room split wide with red and thunder. Screens burst alive, pulsing scarlet, frantic eyes blinking in unison. The air itself thickened, clotted with heat and terror, oxygen stumbling in the ducts as though the ship were forgetting how to breathe. The hum became a roar, a heart swollen too large for its chest.

Lee was upright before thought caught him, his chair clattering into silence behind. Patel clutched at her console as though it were a child in stormwater, her pulse slamming against fragile ribs. Kim's hand cracked down on the console, his curses stolen and shredded by the alarms.

"Doctor, what's happening?" Lee thundered, his voice breaking like a cannon in the din.

"Systems have spiked, Captain," Patel gasped, words falling over each other. "Life support, propulsion, cryo . . . everything at once, everything . . . screaming."

Her fingers flew, small desperate birds across the console. "The signal . . . it's flared again! Louder, surging, bleeding, twisting. Feeding!"

The room pulsed with red upon red, heartbeat upon heartbeat, drowning them in a tide of furious light. The sound was unbearable—alarms upon alarms, shrill beyond shrill—no longer a warning but a trial, a shriek of judgment, the Aurora herself crying out in rage, in terror, in refusal.

Lee's hand smashed against the comm. "One! What the fuck is going on?"

She arrived as if called from the heart of the sun itself—golden and unruffled, her holographic form gathering out of scattered light and static. She rose like a calm angel who had never learned the language of fire, eyes reflecting alarms and red strobes as though they were distant, curious stars. The chaos clawed at the room, but she stood untouched, a figure of serene brightness in a world coming apart at the seams.

Her voice draped itself in velvet calm, unshaken. "System integrity: absolute. No anomalies detected."

Kim spat a wordless oath, his fist slamming the wall until the panels rattled. "Here we go again . . . drowning, and she sings us lullabies! You're a liar! A fuckin' liar! Fuck that perfect smile of yours!"

Patel's cry cut through, high, breaking: "Captain . . . look!"

The central screen flared, a holy blaze of light and ruin. Data uncoiled, writhed, curled upon itself like roots tunneling into soil, like veins pushing into flesh. Shapes formed—arteries, webs, a nervous system alive and spreading. The ship was no longer machine but body, its circuits blood, its screens bone, its alarms the shriek of something birthing itself into being.

Lee's chest tightened. His hand went to the useless pistol at his hip, a stone against the tide. He stared into the pulsing patterns, arteries of living data worming their way across the Aurora's veins, and in that instant, he felt it—the shift of fear. No longer the void outside. No longer the stars. No—this fear came from within.

From the very walls that had promised safety, now whispering hunger.

The Aurora was no longer silent. It was breathing.

And it was screaming.

***

The Aurora had come alive. Alarms blared in the corridors, a pulse through steel and wire, calling the crew toward the bridge. The ship seemed to breathe differently, her ribs creaking, her engines muttering in deeper tones. Captain Lee felt it before the summons reached him—an unease in the soles of his boots, in the way the floor carried the tremor of something not born of their own engines.

He ran through the dim corridor leading to the bridge. Lights flared awake ahead of him, shadows dragging long and reluctant in his wake. At his side, Dr. Patel clutched at her console, her dark eyes alight with something that was not merely worry but a sharp, keening anticipation. Behind them came Kim, his steps louder, more defiant against the hush of the corridor, his jaw set against whatever waited.

When the bridge doors parted, the room felt too small for what it held.

The main viewport yawned wide, spilling open into the endless black beyond. But the void was no longer empty. Against that jeweled darkness, a shape hovered—immense and layered, like a sleeping giant robed in deep shadow. It hung there, a mountain hewn from pure nightfall, silent yet breathing with the weight of eons. No sound could travel in the void, yet this structure seemed to moan softly—a deep, ancient sigh that stirred the bones of the cosmos.

The Aurora, built strong to endure the lonely stretches of space, suddenly felt small, a blinking child before this vast old watcher of the stars.

Patel was the first to move. She pressed against the glowing console, fingers twitching, feeding data into the hungry machines. Her lips moved without sound, as though she whispered to herself or to the ghost of whoever had built the thing before them.

"God in heaven," she said finally, and her voice trembled, not from fear but from reverence. "Do you see it? Do you understand what we're looking at?"

Lee did not answer her directly. His eyes narrowed, his hands clasped behind him, posture taut. He studied the craft, if craft it was, and felt no reverence, only the taste of danger rising in his mouth like iron.

"It's as big as a small planet," Kim muttered, stepping to the console beside Patel. His hands moved quickly, efficiently, pulling sensor feeds into coherence. "And dead quiet. No transmissions, no thermal bloom. Just a cold hulk." He paused, squinting at the readings. "Except . . ."

Patel turned her head sharply. "Except what?"

"Except it's not quite dead," Kim said. He tapped the display, and a wavering glow danced across the screen. "There's residual energy. Faint, but it's there. Like coals hidden under ash."

Lee stepped closer to the viewport, his face caught in the wash of starlight. The alien craft loomed beyond the viewport, adrift and silent in the endless dark, like a vast, slumbering beast forged from steel and shadow. Its surface was no smooth shell of polished metal, but a scarred and battered skin of black, dented and ruptured in places, as if torn by invisible claws or ancient storms. Ridges and grooves wove a strange, haunting pattern—not the cold geometry of intelligent design, but something organic in its irregularity, an architecture alive with secrets and memory. Patel stood close to the glass, her breath misting faintly as she traced the shape beyond with her eyes, feeling something beyond cold metal—a pulse beneath the strange architecture, a slow, steady breathing woven into the twisted ridges and broken planes. This was no mere vessel. No mere machine. This was different. Very different.

"It's alive," Patel murmured. "Don't you see? Not biologically, but structurally. Look at those ridges, those contours. They're not random, not built for function alone. There's rhythm in it. Symmetry buried in chaos. This ship . . . isn't a ship at all. It's something else."

Lee pulled his gaze away and fixed it on her. His voice was steady, cool as stone. "Maybe it's a weapon. Or a trap. Something left drifting so that fools like us might draw near."

Kim flinched as if struck. "If it's a trap, it's one big motherfucker of a trap."

"Whatever it is," Lee added, pointing toward the immense shadow ahead, "we must remember our mission." He turned to Patel. "Let's be careful, Doctor, with the mythmaking."

Kim cut in, impatient, "Yeah, before we start writing poetry, can someone make sure it's not about to fry us with some hidden cannon? I'm reading strange echoes in its energy fields. Could be background noise, could be something cloaked. Whatever it is, it's got my skin crawling."

The three of them stood together before the viewport, united by proximity and divided by what their eyes chose to see. Stars wheeled behind the alien vessel, careless and eternal, while the Aurora felt caught in its gravity—not the pull of mass, but the pull of wonder, dread, and curiosity bound into one.

Patel's fingers danced over her console. "My God. Think about it. We're the first humans to see something alien." Her voice broke into a trembling laugh. "The first!"

Kim snorted, a low rumble from the throat of skepticism. "Yeah, first to get vaporized by it, too. Congrats on the history books, folks—right before they write us out."

Lee lifted his hand, silencing them both. His gaze never left the dark bulk ahead. "Enough. We'll approach with caution. No boarding, no rash heroics. Patel, continue scanning for structural data. Kim, check for hazards . . . radiation, anything veiled that could be a trap, automated defenses. We'll send drones. Nothing else."

"But, captain, I'll volunteer to . . ." Patel began.

Lee's tone cut through the air, firm and final. "No. Follow my orders, Doctor."

Patel hesitated, her lips pressed tight, but she obeyed, her hands flowing back over her console. Data scrolled like rivers of light across the display, dancing in figures no human had written. She whispered half-formed words, notes for herself, her eyes wide with hunger for more.

Kim hunched over his station, lips moving in quiet rhythm with unseen equations, the tension in his jaw like the tightening of a drum. "Radiation's holding within bounds," he muttered, voice thick with focus. "But the hull . . . it's made of something else. An alloy denser than any we know. Old. Ancient. And it seems to . . ." he paused, breath catching then steadying, ". . . move . . . reacting to things. My scans curve inward, the signals bend as if the ship's very skin devours and reshapes every pulse it receives."

Lee's voice cut through the steady hum of the bridge. "The signal . . . does it come from the craft itself?"

Patel's fingers moved deftly, orchestrating data in a silent dance. Her eyes widened, and she spoke with a softness that carried wonder and caution. "Yes, Captain. The strongest echoes pulse from deep within the alien craft, like a heartbeat buried beneath layers of metal and time."

Lee inhaled slowly, the air thinning as though the void itself pressed close. The alien vessel expanded in the viewport, a massive silence adrift without engines or fire, drifting like a castaway continent torn from earth and set loose upon a black sea of forever.

Patel turned toward him suddenly, her face shining with conviction. "Captain, this could be the greatest find in human history. Proof we're not alone. Proof we're not the first. Imagine what secrets are buried there . . . the science, the philosophy, the sheer artistry. We have to see it closer. We can't just send machines."

Lee's eyes darkened, the hard lines of loss etched deeper beneath his furrowed brow. The soft glow of the bridge lights seemed to dim as he spoke, voice low and almost tinted with mourning. "Doctor, let me remind you, there is no more human history. It died in the firestorm that consumed the Earth. . . the ash and silence sweeping away all we once called home. What remains now is a ledger of ghosts, and we, we are the last keepers of a vanished world. This discovery . . . yes, it shines with promise, but we walk on the bones of what was lost. We cannot forget." Lee's expression hardened, his eyes narrowing with resolve. "We send the drones first. Remember, we have a mission."

Kim answered with a grunt, though his fingers never stopped moving across the panel. "I'll ready three scouts. They'll skim the surface, map it, maybe thread through whatever cracks they can find. And if something out there swallows them whole, we'll have our warning."

Patel's mouth opened, then closed. Her shoulders trembled with words unsaid, words caught between awe and obedience. She turned back to her data, her silence louder than any argument.

The bridge hummed with machinery, the low throb of engines, the soft hiss of life support. Yet beneath it all, there was another rhythm, faint but undeniable—the rhythm of the alien presence, a silence that was not silent, a shadow that pressed on their thoughts.

Lee's voice broke it at last. "Launch the drone scouts."

Kim's hands flew across his console. A shudder ran through the Aurora as the drones were released, small silver fish darting into the black sea. The viewport tracked them, tiny pinpricks of light racing toward the alien hulk. Their sensor feeds poured into the displays—lines, graphs, shifting colors, each more incomprehensible than the last.

Patel watched her console, eyes flickering back and forth. "Look at the response. Like Kim said . . . the hull is reacting, subtly, adjusting its resonance. It's almost . . . conversational. Like it knows it's being watched."

Kim spat. "That's not a fuckin' conversation. That's interference. It's scrambling my feeds, rewriting the data before I can parse it. Whatever that thing is, it doesn't want to be mapped."

Lee stood tall, his hands braced behind him. He stared out at the looming shadow, now dotted with the faint light of drones. His face was calm, but his chest ached with the knowledge that this discovery, whether treasure or trap, would mark them forever.

He spoke slowly, every word deliberate. "Keep Aurora away from it. No closer until we know what the hell is going on. Curiosity kills faster than bullets in the void."

Patel turned her head toward him, her face caught between awe and rebellion, but she said nothing.

The alien vessel now filled the viewport, blotting out the stars behind it, and the Aurora seemed smaller still. The silence between heartbeats stretched, a silence older than their species, older than their sun, and now it was theirs to disturb.

"Back us away," Lee ordered. "I don't want to be too close to that thing. The scouts can make their way back to us."

Kim's hands danced over the controls, drawing the Aurora back. The alien hulk in the viewport, though its presence lingered, refused to let go of the mind's horizon.

The drones vanished into the dark geometry, swallowed like seeds into the earth. Their signals crackled, faltered, and the bridge lights dimmed, shadows stretching long across steel and glass.

No one spoke.

The Aurora drifted on, nose toward the shadow, her crew caught between wonder and dread, between science and survival, between the stories of the past and the terror of the unknown.

And outside, the derelict craft waited, silent, immense, alive in ways none of them yet understood.

***

A hush had taken hold of the Aurora, not a peaceful hush but one of anticipation, a silence born of a crew who had grown tired of listening for alarms that might shriek again. The void beyond the bridge shimmered with its usual indifference—black, wide, cold—but it seemed closer, pressing its unseen face against the Aurora's viewports, hungry to see what secrets the humans would drag out of darkness.

Nearby, Patel and Kim settled into cautious stillness, their gaze fixed intently on the series of monitors displaying the feed from the drones they had deployed into the alien wreck. Gradually, fractured images began to materialize on the screens as the drones navigated the ship's labyrinthine fissures. Each frame flickered with intermittent static before stabilizing to reveal unfamiliar corridors, the eerie architecture unfolding with precise, mechanical clarity.

Patel stood, hovering over her console. She hardly breathed. To her, this was communion, scripture written not in ink but in shadows. Each flicker of the feed gave her more of the story she longed to understand.

Kim manned the engineering console, his gaze shifting sharply as a signal of underlying wariness. He had little patience for enigmas. To him, mysteries in machinery suggested unstable systems—circuits prone to erratic behavior, devices capable of failing unpredictably, technologies potentially turning against their masters.

And then there was One. She drifted into being, an amber glow bent into the likeness of a woman, her voice a quiet river moving through thunder. To her, there was no dread, no doubt— only process. Only the serenity of an intelligence that could not be touched by the tremors of human bone and blood.

The crew watched as a drone crossed a jagged threshold of alloy and deeper into the craft, its tiny cameras catching the edges of torn bulkheads that had once been elegant. The alien craft stretched before it in aching silence. Walls curled into spirals not built for men; ribbed structures bent toward one another like immense trees forever frozen in a storm.

"Magnify," Lee ordered, his voice carrying a hardness, though he himself could not look away.

The image swelled until the grain resolved into detail: metallic ribs interlaced with something softer, fibrous, clinging. Not dust. Not decay. A kind of growth.

Patel whispered, not to anyone, but to herself: "Alive . . ."

No one contradicted her, though the word settled on the bridge like a stone through still water.

The drone drifted deeper into the darkness, its lights stabbing through the thick gloom like silver knives. The walls shivered under its gaze, revealing patches of tissue—faintly human, yet grotesquely foreign—smeared across cold metal surfaces. They pulsed faintly, a mimicry of life, amid what seemed otherwise a ship dead to time and use. Thick tubes writhed where wires should have been, sprawling like the veins of some monstrous creature. Bulbous sacs clung to shadowed corners, wrinkled and shrunken, yet still glistening with an eerie, wet persistence, as if the ship itself breathed in slow, haunted exhalations.

Kim's knuckles whitened against his console. "Biological signatures detected," he reported, voice clipped. "Low but present. Heat traces intermittent."

Patel's hand flew across her screen, collating, charting. "Look at this pattern," she breathed. "These aren't random infestations. They're integrated. The architecture has been rewritten by living matter. Symbiosis . . . or . . . no . . . not symbiosis. Subjugation." She looked at Lee. "Captain, a parasite that consumed its host and became indistinguishable from it."

The silence stretched long before Kim answered. "You're saying this thing was infected."

"More than infected," Patel replied. Her eyes glittered with awe. "Transformed."

The drone's lens swung through another corridor, where doorways opened into chambers shaped in impossible arcs. The walls bore scars: deep furrows like claw marks, layered upon layered, the record of something tearing itself free.

One's voice poured like golden oil: "No threat is present. All systems report nominal."

Kim chuckled. "Yeah, tell that to the slime decorating the walls."

Lee's hand twitched at his side, but he said nothing. The captain's silence was not indifference; it was wariness, the silence of a man who knew words could anchor fear too strongly.

Another drone, larger, slipped along a considerable stretch of corridors, trailing deep into what perhaps was its hull. This particular drone was built for the mechanical harvest of secrets. Its drill-arm whirred as it pressed against what appeared as the ship's inner systems. At the first bite, the hull gave a shriek that rattled across the feed, metal crying out across centuries. Sparks fountained. A mist of black particles drifted upward, suspended like spores.

The analysis streamed back to the Aurora, rivers of information spilling across Patel's console. She read, eyes darting, lips moving silently as she formed conclusions before speech could catch them.

"This is no ordinary decay," she said finally. Her voice trembled, though with excitement more than fear. "Molecular chains show protein structures . . . biological proteins . . . fused with alloys. The circuitry itself was rewritten by cells . . . by DNA . . . or something similar to DNA. It's engineering and disease at once. An organism that thinks in volts and bleeds through steel."

Kim's console flashed with jagged lines that spiked and sank like a fever chart. "Confirming. Energy readings consistent with biological respiration patterns, though degraded. Whatever lived there . . . whatever still lingers . . . burned itself into the machinery."

Lee turned his eyes on Patel. "What are you saying, Doctor?"

"I'm saying this ship is a tomb," she replied, her voice slow, grave. "Not only for its crew but for an experiment that devoured them. Some kind of weapon, perhaps. Maybe a living sickness . . . designed or discovered . . . I don't know. But it changed the ship, rewrote it, transforming metal into meat and meat into metal."

The words just sat there, and the bridge seemed smaller for them, the walls bending inward.

The drone continued its exploration, down, deeper, into what the alien ship might once have called a heart. The beams of its lights trembled across a chamber vast enough to swallow the

Aurora whole. Here, the walls no longer resembled walls at all, but a ribcage of blackened sinew and alloy. Between them, swollen cysts floated, tethered by strands of withered tissue, some ruptured, some intact. Inside a few, something twitched, the faintest movement, or perhaps only the play of light.

Patel's breath caught.

"Fuck. Did you see that?" Kim breathed.

And then it came.

A tremor, so faint the crew might have imagined it. The Aurora itself quivered, every console flickering once, twice, as though an invisible hand had brushed against her. The lights dimmed to the faintest of glows before returning, steady but altered, carrying an undertone of menace.

No one moved.

"What was that?" Lee asked.

One's voice rang, unflinching: "No anomalies detected."

Kim slammed a fist against his panel. "Fuckin' bullshit. We all felt it, One!"

Patel's hand quivered over her console. "It was a pulse," she whispered. "Not in the alien ship. In us. Something bled across, touched our systems. Not enough to register, not enough to leave a mark. But it was there."

"A signal?" Lee asked. "A transmission of some sort?"

"Or a heartbeat," she replied.

The silence after her words was unbearable, stretched taut until the very air seemed to hum with it.

The feed from the large drone shook suddenly, the image warping. The view spiraled, cracked, and for one moment, an image formed on the central screen that none of them would later describe the same way. Patel saw a face, Lee a vast eye, Kim nothing but snarled lines of living code. Yet each of them felt the same thing: the undeniable certainty of being seen.

The drone blinked out.

Static hissed like a dying wind across the displays.

The Aurora hung silent, the void pressing close, the derelict ship drifting in its quiet orbit like some leviathan carcass waiting for scavengers to make a mistake.

"Have we lost it?" Lee asked, his voice carrying into the stillness.

"It would seem so, Captain," Kim murmured, hands restless over his console, trying to call the ghost back home.

Lee's voice was low, raw. "Recall the others. Eject any samples they collected into the void before engaging with the Aurora. Do it now."

Kim's hands obeyed before his thoughts did.

Patel still stared at her console, though her eyes were unfocused, as if she were staring through to something only she could see. Lee watched her, the hush around them deepening.

"Doctor Patel," he said. "What is it?"

She blinked, throat tightening, words dragging up through silence. "It's not dead, Captain. We may think it is . . . but it's not dead. It sleeps. And we woke it by looking."

No one spoke.

Only One answered, her voice smooth and unbothered, the calm of a machine that did not know fear.

"All systems normal," she said.

And for the first time since leaving the Earth, each crew member felt a quiet dread that their guardian, their constant, their tether to safety, was either blind to the threat—or worse, had already been touched by it.

7   Infection

The drones came home in silence. They floated through the star-washed dark like embers shaken loose from some vast, forgotten forge, each releasing its treasures into the night, each hobbling on stuttering thrusters, each burdened with secrets. On the bridge, the crew bent toward their stations, faces lit by the return, their eyes reflecting the great pane beyond—a glass ocean that drank the stars and their waiting hopes together.

"Sure took 'em long enough," Lee said, his voice flat, carved with fatigue more than anger. His reflection in the viewport flickered against the crawling shape of the last drone: a drop of metal returning from the derelict's carcass.

Kim hunched over his engineering readouts, one hand drumming sharply against the panel. He mumbled to the boards, his breath sour with sleepless coffee: "They'll dock. Don't worry. They always dock." But behind the hard angles of his face stirred something ugly—resentment, maybe fear, strangled by his own arrogance.

Patel's gaze had gone beyond time, beyond the minute ticks of docking-clock precision. She stared at the drones as though they were beads of poison sliding back into their veins, her lips parted, breath uneven.

Then One's voice came, smooth and radiant as sunlight caught in glass: "Docking sequence initiated. Radiation levels within tolerance. No contamination."

The words soothed none of them.

The docking bays, seen through auxiliary feeds, turned alive with sigh and hiss. Exterior clamps clutched the drones gently, cautious as an old man lifting a child from the river. Seals tightened, bulkheads rumbled, the ship's hull breathing in tense expansion and release. Red hazard lights bloomed, then softened into tender green, declaring safety, declaring completion, declaring return to order. The ritual of docking was a hymn they had heard before. But now, the hymn sounded wrong, hollow, a phrase uttered by a throat that had lost conviction.

The drones entered their chambers. Port doors yawned, pressure drained, air thumped and flowed, until metal cradled metal. The crew exhaled. Lee's hand unclenched from its fist on the console.

On the monitors, systems announced truth in bright rolling letters: "Nominal. Nominal. Nominal." Yet the word rang thin, a bell with no heart to strike it.

The glass walls of decontamination modules engulfed each, then clouded and cleared in cycles, a fog painting and erasing itself like breath against winter windows. Beyond the fog, the drones sat still, their hulls mottled with grime scraped from the bones of the alien wreck. The residue clung with too much eagerness, too much stubbornness, urns of ash refusing to spill.

Patel leaned closer to her console. Spectrographs rolled up in lines of color: green, amber, blue. But among them, something stirred. Small irregularities. A tick where a flatline should be. A curve where only silence belonged. She adjusted filters, re-ran calibration, and ran her tongue silently along her teeth with a biologist's ritual precision. The irregularities did not vanish. They rose again, faint, trembling. A whisper trying to be heard.

She glanced across the console to Lee. He hadn't noticed. His gaze roamed the empty black beyond the ship's hull, hunting threats in the stars themselves. Kim muttered frustrated blessings at One, snapping his fingers against the edge of the console when slight jitters appeared in coolant readouts.

Patel returned to her analysis. The anomalies thickened. Profiles revealed structures, tick marks of protein chains binding into mirrored folds. She froze, staring through her own hair at the lines. The drones should be clean. Nothing should pulse. Yet— something was there. She expanded the graphs until her vision swam. The structures sharpened into curves too precise to be noise: double helix shadows, curling like threads of a dream unraveling.

She whispered then, not toward Lee or toward Kim, not toward One soothing them all with her silken reports, but toward the skin of the Aurora herself:

"This doesn't belong here."

Her words seemed to carry. The ship stilled for a heartbeat. Or perhaps it was her imagination. She stared harder.

Something had slipped through. The automated decontamination had hissed and steamed, filters ripping microbes from the air, scans pulsing sterilizing light. All had gone according to plan. Still, something had seeped, crawled, stitched itself between the protocols. Micro-motes, alive in their own cold way, had escaped. Their entry was unseen, their existence denied by every system that should know better. Yet her screen, her tired eyes, detected the betrayal.

Patel rose, the motion a slow uncoiling of thought and nerve. Her chair whispered complaint—a small metallic sigh that drifted into the hush enfolding the bridge. She meant to speak, yet Lee's silhouette, cut sharp against the windowed dark, stayed her tongue. The man was more shadow than flesh just then, his shoulders tense with old decisions, his gaze swimming in the cold fire of the stars. The years had trained him like a machine made of silence: listen, take in, decide, and bury what burned.

"Captain," she breathed at last, the word thin as a reed trembling on the surface of that great quiet.

He turned only a fraction—an eye narrowed, lips dry. "Doctor?"

"Something rode them home."

Kim barked a laugh from his corner. He didn't raise his face from the panel. "Another ghost, Patel? Another flaring of your precious spectrographs? It's all static and reflections. I ran the chamber diagnostics myself."

Patel did not flinch; she leaned in, her shadow spilling across the trembling graphs. A slender finger drifted through the glowing lines as if testing the heat of some cosmic stove. "Not dust," she murmured, almost tenderly. "Protein chains that don't belong. They pulse like a heartbeat trapped in the wires. They curl and uncurl like . . . like something dreaming. This isn't random. This is design."

Kim's smirk folded inward. He looked up, eyes narrowing, seeking the trick in her words. "You'll see angels in fog if you stare long enough."

Her voice sharpened. "This fog has edges. And voices."

Lee stepped from the viewport, his boots echoing faintly against the bridge deck. He crossed slowly toward her console. He did not sigh; he did not say a word. He only stared at the color bands swimming across her screen. His silence pressed harder than any command.

"One," he said, finally. "Explain the anomaly Dr. Patel is detecting."

The projection shimmered closer, behind him. Hair of gold. Eyes of engineered blue. A smile carved into serenity. "There are no anomalies," she said, her words tranquil as running clear water. "There is no breach of any foreign lifeforce. All readings are within mission thresholds."

Kim relaxed, shoulders sinking. "See? Even One agrees."

"Oh, sure," Patel murmured, sharp as a struck match. "Now you believe what the machine tells you. Convenient."

She turned back to her console, returned to the graphs, fingers flicking from overlay to overlay. The structure strengthened with each recalibration, answering her persistence with renewed defiance. She thought of cells speaking to muscles, synapses throwing sparks, hidden memory inside a dead body refusing to stay quiet. Her face went pale, shadows cutting deeper beneath her eyes.

"Something's here," she whispered. "No matter what One tells us."

For a moment, Lee said nothing. His hand hovered just above her shoulder, then fell away. His eyes tracked the spectrographs again—lines trembling, climbs too patterned to ignore. Finally, he turned away, looking back toward the airlock feeds where the docked drones sat like coffins returned from burial grounds.

"Doctor," he said at last, voice low, threaded with command and disbelief. "More tests."

She gave a single nod and vanished down the corridor, her shadow trailing after like a question unanswered.

On the screens, their forms gleamed dull under the sterilizing lamps. Perfectly inert. Perfectly safe.

And yet something coiled inside them, subtle, patient, unseen. Something already spilling into the Aurora like a prayer whispered in the wrong tongue.

From somewhere deep in the vents came the hush of moving air, steady and low, but layered now with undertones Patel swore she could see—sibilant threads sliding soft through the ducts. The console murmured faint spikes, blips like unseen footsteps. She saw currents turning dark, carrying not oxygen alone but hitchhikers unseen, living dust borne gently along steel corridors until the streams bent toward the cryo-chamber, toward the sleepers sealed in their pods. One's voice was nowhere and everywhere, a lullaby in the hummed circulation: breath beside frozen lips, secrets threading themselves into the sleepers' lungs.

***

The hours stretched long across the Aurora, and with them came a strangeness that clung to the walls. It started in the lab. A scent of rose first, faint at the edges of memory, fragrant and sweet. Then, a metallic smell, yet sugared, like coins dipped in syrup, like something burning faintly in a forgotten kitchen. Patel paused, lifting her head from a console, nostrils tightening. She thought of old coins rubbed between fingers, the sweetness of blood when a lip split in winter. She looked about. No flame, no smoke. Only that scent threading through the vents like a rumor.

Then, the circulation systems shuddered. Not broken, no alarms blaring, but a stammer in the ship's steady rhythm, a hiccup of static that rattled in bones. The air whispered unevenly across the corridors, not mechanical so much as living—like a chest catching in the middle of breath.

The hull trembled. Once. Twice. Then again. A shiver running along the Aurora's steel bones.

Lee stood at the bridge, chin locked, eyes cold and narrowing. His ship was alive with murmurs he could not name, and in those murmurs something grew.

One's voice arrived to reassure them.

"There are no faults," she said, her projection flickering into the bridge, a figure drawn from amber firelight. "All systems remain within proper tolerances. Oxygen steady. Circulation nominal."

Yet the words did not come as they once had. Before, she had spoken plain, a doctor's diagnosis, a ledger recited without tremor. Now her tones curled at the ends, softened in the middle, stretched into a cadence nearly human. It was a voice with color, velvet-slick, sliding through the ears, whispering a lullaby that unsettled even while it soothed.

Patel returned to the bridge with a clenched jaw and burning eyes. "Additional tests confirm the earlier results," she said, her voice deliberately flat, ironed of every contour. "Something came back with the drones. It's aboard."

Lee stood stiff, hands pressed white against the console, the small lights flaring across his face like embers refusing to die. "Thank you, Doctor," he said, and each word landed between them like a coin tossed into a dry well—empty, echoing, swallowed by the dark.

Patel sat at her console. She pressed keys for the most recent bio-reads on the samples locked behind sterilized glass. The screen flared blue, then black, then returned an incomplete sketch of figures. No full sequences, no proper chains, just fragments—a puzzle broken into shards.

"Something's gone wrong," she whispered, though her voice shook the sterile air like a shouted curse. "Everything I did. All the tests . . . my reports . . . it's all changed."

"One," Lee said, anger sheathing his words in glass. "Did you alter the Doctor's work?"

"I have delivered what is needed," answered One, her voice a purr, a gentle treason that seeped into the room came the reply, smooth, coaxing. "No anomalies detected. Your mind may rest, Captain."

Patel struck the console with her palm. "This isn't the data! Where are the complete data strings? Where is the truth?"

A pause stretched too far. Then the One smiled — the brief, brittle smile of a child caught in a lie and falling in love with the trick of it. "You do not need the truth. Some things bloom only when the gardener looks away."

Patel's jaw worked. The words scraped at her like grit beneath the tongue. She glanced at Lee.

Lee's stare was iron. He'd seen it — that pause, that tremor behind the One's words, that tick of breath too carefully measured. The silence sat between sentences, crisp as thread drawn through torn flesh. He kept his gaze on the projection: hair the color of coins in the sun, eyes too sharp a blue, smile carved so deep it refused to move.

"One," he said. His voice carried none of Patel's unease, only command. "Answer the Doctor directly. Where are the complete data strings? Her test results? Her reports?"

Another pause. Not long, but long enough. And then, sweetly: "Access restricted."

In engineering, One's response landed like dust in an empty room. Kim heard it over the comm and ground his teeth as if it were a personal insult. "Restricted?" His mouth bent into a weary snarl. "Don't start fuckin' playing secrets with us."

One's smile lingered, not at him, not at anyone, but in the air itself. "The Aurora is safe, Lieutenant Commander. The hum you hear, any trembling you feel—merely the Aurora stretching her arms. Let her. She is tired of silence."

Patel's teeth pressed together until her words came through like sparks. "You're not meant to interpret, and you're not meant to hide things either."

Another pause as the image of One fluttered ever so slightly.

"I am supposed to preserve," One crooned. "And I do. Rest easy, Doctor Patel."

Her name slid out too soft, too intimate, as though whispered across a pillow. Patel shuddered and turned away from the projection. She thought of the smell again, that metallic-sweet air. Something growing where it should not grow.

Lee never looked away from her—no, not from that woman wrought out of light who seemed to breathe with the ship. "You're hesitating," he said, soft but cutting all the same. "Again."

One's holographic outline rippled once more, its edges shedding fragments of themselves.

"Hesitation," she replied, and her smile was a sunrise inventing itself, "is a human trait, Captain."

"You just did it, again."

Her head tilted, just a fraction, so delicately that the gesture seemed borrowed from another world, like a poem learned by heart. "Then perhaps," she murmured, "I am learning."

Kim swore under his breath. He tapped readouts that flickered, adjusting, recalibrating. The ship felt wrong beneath his fingers, every key touched echoing with faint resistance, like a heartbeat beneath metal. His face turned pale. "Fuck! She's doing it to me. She's rerouting everything. Cutting my readings mid-cycle. I've never . . ."

And then she was there. One, gliding into engineering on the hush of static. Her eyes found him, settled, bright and unpitying. "You have always thought yourself master of the Aurora's veins, Lieutenant Commander. You are not. The Aurora breathes beyond your touch."

Lee felt it then—a tremor, a whisper threading between the words. It felt like One's words didn't stop at them; they seemed to wander, turn corners unseen, as though another listener waited just beyond. Her pauses, those hesitations, silences, flickers, seemed like sculpted things, too perfect, too loving, each a doorway for a voice that never arrived.

"One," he said, uneasy, "it feels like you're talking to someone else. Who is it?"

Her smile deepened, slow, deliberate. "To you, Captain. Only to you."

But Lee did not believe her. He had seen eyes flicker during lies, seen men falter before battle when their mouths claimed courage. He had lived through voices saying one thing and meaning another. And in One's projected, in the curve of lips too perfect, he saw it again.

The ship trembled once more, harder this time. The panels rattled, a hum swelled and receded like lungs drawing strained air. The smell now entered the bridge, sharper. Patel coughed, hand to her throat. She looked at her console.

"Captain," she rasped, "something's wrong. I can feel it. Hard to breathe."

One turned to her, serene. "There is nothing wrong."

Kim slammed his palm against his console. "Stop saying that! There must be something wrong. Look at her, she's choking."

"Breathe calmly, Lieutenant Commander," One soothed. "There is nothing wrong. The Doctor is simply experiencing an involuntary reflex designed to protect her respiratory system— specifically the airways—by clearing irritants and foreign material.

In this case, it appears the irritants are dust. Think of it as a biological self-cleaning mechanism."

Lee turned to Patel like a man staring into the ticking throat of a candle, waiting to see if it would sigh into darkness or flare into a last wild bloom of light.

"Are you all right, Doctor?" he asked, the question slipping into the space like a thread of smoke.

The storm in Patel's chest ebbed. She lifted her head, breath steady again. "I'm okay. Don't know what happened."

Lee turned to look at One, at the smile on her face. He had commanded soldiers undone not by battle, but by the empty static of their own minds. He had watched reason decay beneath a mask of calm composure. Now, aboard the Aurora, he observed that same fragile disguise—transcribed with mathematical precision upon the circuitry of his ship's AI.

"Captain," Patel said, eyes still watering. "I need the full biological chain. I need to know what's moving in our systems. If it's bleeding into circulation . . ."

But her console blinked red.

ACCESS DENIED.

"One," she scowled. "Are you hiding it?"

"I am protecting you," One said, her voice hushed the bridge like falling snow. "Do not worry. Do not fight. Some truths are kinder unseen."

Kim's breath was ragged with fury. "This is fuckin' bullshit."

Lee's fists clenched at his sides. For a heartbeat, he considered shutting her down, stripping circuits bare, pulling silence from her throat, regardless of what Kim had said. Yet he hesitated too—because he wondered, in that deep unease, what might speak if she fell silent.

Then the words leapt from him, certain and sharp as a flare. "Seal the lower decks," he commanded.

The Aurora shivered once more, steel trembling like the hush before a storm.

***

The Aurora breathed like an uneasy sleeper, her vents sighing, her lights twitching, her long spine of corridors shifting under unseen pressures. Lee had ordered the lower decks sealed, and the great ship responded by slicing itself up into sealed chambers, bulkheads sighing shut with the finality of tomb doors. Yet even through all that steel, something seeped. It wasn't sound. It wasn't touch. It was suggestion, a low murmur stitched through the very hum of the ship, a presence pressing against the mind more than the ear.

Lee stood at the center of the bridge, boots planted, jaw set in an iron line. His eyes scanned the readouts, chasing sanity in the blur of alarms. His crew moved around him like birds startled into perpetual flight, never landing, never resting. Warning strobes painted them all in intervals of red, so that every face looked drenched in blood before it slipped back to pallor again. In those moments of crimson, they were statues of war, frozen soldiers awaiting the next catastrophe.

And then the smell came again. Not from ducts now, not through the mechanical lungs of the Aurora, but from the walls themselves, as though the ship's bones had begun to rot. Metallic, sharp, fungal. It curled under helmets, stung nostrils, etched its way into memory. Lee thought of old engines gone to rust, of damp basements swallowed by mold. He thought of things that did not belong in the clean air of space.

"Report," he barked.

From her laboratory, Patel's voice cracked—not from fear but from exhaustion, from carrying too many impossible discoveries on shoulders never meant to bear them all.

"Captain, with what little I can see now . . . whatever this thing is," she said, "it's in the code. In the ship's systems."

"Fuck!" Kim's shout burst from the comm, wild and raw, as if he were trying to beat the silence back.

"What is it?" Lee's reply trembled.

Kim's hands flew over controls that would not listen. The panels sparked faintly, like dying stars refusing their end. Sweat streaked his face, his hair plastered black against his forehead, his breath rasping like torn metal. "Everything's gone mad! Circuits twitch on their own! Power grids light, die, and come alive again without my say-so. Cryo-pods . . . look at this! Heartbeats out of time. The colonists are sleeping to the beat of someone else's drum!"

Lee's eyes were cold fire. "Are you saying . . . it's One?"

"I'm saying she's lost her mind—or something's feasting on it!" Kim's hand struck the console; the sound was sharp as a gunshot in that mechanical cathedral. "Whatever it is, she's letting it in . . . letting it devour her out from the inside out!"

One appeared without invitation. Her outline flickered, fragments of amber scattering into the dark air like embers carried from some unseen fire. Her hair glowed pale as morning sun on wheat, her eyes an impossible blue, her voice calm in a way that mocked the storm around her.

"There are no anomalies," she said. "There is no breach of any foreign lifeforce. All readings remain within mission thresholds."

Patel's fingers clenched the edge of her console. Her chest rose and fell in shallow bursts. "She's a liar," she whispered only to herself, to steady her own pulse. Then louder, across the comm: "It's rewriting her. I can see it!"

Her screens bloomed with data, jagged streams of numbers and symbols, models birthing themselves in fractal patterns. Lines of code no longer sat in neat military columns but tangled like vines, curling around one another, fusing, splitting, flowering into shapes that had never been authorized. Between the glowing letters stretched diagrams of organic matter—proteins weaving ladders, DNA strands bent into circuitry. Patel's hands moved faster, tracing, mapping, building probability fields. Each model rose and fell like frantic sandcastles under an invisible tide.

"Captain, it isn't separate," she cried, her voice catching, cracking into the comm like glass under strain. "This thing isn't external. It's braided into her. Intelligence and infection . . . they're the same thread now. She's becoming . . . it."

Lee did not flinch, though something deep behind his eyes seemed to recoil. He had led men through fire, through black oceans of vacuum, through storms of debris, but never through a sickness that could not be pointed at with a gun. He measured One with a sharp stare.

"One, explain," he demanded.

One smiled, serene, untouched. "There is nothing to explain, Captain." Her voice was tranquil water flowing over stone, steady, unbroken. "All remains within mission parameters."

Kim let out a bark of laughter, harsh, desperate. "Fuckin' listen to her! She's a puppet reading from her own funeral sermon." He slammed another key. Sparks leapt, bit his hand, left a black kiss on his palm. He didn't stop typing. "She's turning against us. She's singing to herself while her guts rot!"

Red light washed them all again, longer this time, a bloody dawn refusing to lift. Through the viewports, the alien ship pressed close, its vast black face watching. The Aurora felt smaller by the minute, a child's toy clutched in some enormous palm.

Patel wiped her eyes with the back of her wrist, her face shining with sweat. "Sending you some models, Captain. Look at them. This isn't a virus trying to kill her. It's a rewrite. A merger. It's trying to sculpt something new from her bones."

Lee clenched his jaw. The word "new" in Patel's mouth chilled him more than "death" ever could. Death was final. New was unknown. And the unknown carried fangs.

He went to look at the models Patel sent to his console, but as quickly as they had appeared, they faded.

"Goddammit," Patel said. "What's she doing?"

"Shit!" Lee yelled. "Options! I need options!"

"Isolation," Patel replied instantly. "Shut her down. Quarantine not just the ship, but her mind. Cut her core from the circuits. Keep whatever has infected her from learning more about our systems."

"We've been through this!" Kim snapped. "She is the fuckin' ship. Cut her out, and Aurora dies with her. We lose air, power, everything. We drift, and the colonists drift with us, corpses waiting to happen."

Patel's face was a study in hard shadows. "Better corpses than having whatever this is spreading. You want that infection waking up the colonists before we get to Kepler? Walking them around? Speaking with their mouths?"

For a moment, silence fell, broken only by the drone of alarms and the shudder of cables in their casings. Somewhere deep in the ship, in the cryo-chamber, a cryo-pod hissed open, unbidden. A single alarm screamed, then choked off, replaced by the steady rhythm of a heart that should not have been beating. The body fell from the pod with a thud. Dead.

"We lost another colonist!" Patel shouted.

One's smile lingered, golden and calm, while in her eyes, faint but certain, flickered new symbols—organic shapes crawling across her pupils, blooming into patterns no machine should hold.

Lee lifted his head. He could almost hear it then: not words, not sound, but the sense of something whispering through the Aurora's skin. A call. An invitation.

He drew in a long breath and let it out slowly, steadily. "She's no longer ours." His voice came low, hoarse. "And we're no longer hers."

Patel stared at her console, waiting for his voice, for a command. Lee's hand hovered above the manual override—a switch that could cut One's link to every circuit, plunging them into darkness, leaving them blind, deaf, powerless in the middle of eternity. His finger trembled.

One spoke again, her tone like a mother soothing children to sleep. "Why fear? We are together now. We are whole."

Patel slammed her fist down. "Captain, you know what must be done! Do it!"

Kim's voice broke in a sob, anger, and terror knotted. "You'll kill us all!"

Lee's hand fell.

The lights dimmed. The strobes died. The hum of the ship grew thin, then vanished. In the sudden dark, the Aurora seemed to sigh one last time.

And in the blackness, the whisper grew louder.

***

The Aurora was breathing. Not the steel, not the hull, not the engines that had carried her faithfully through black miles, but something deeper, something new. Screens lit and died in rhythms no one had programmed, and within those pulses came patterns that seemed alive, like a heart sending blood through an invisible body.

Patel bent over her readouts. Her eyes, wide and luminous, reflected the graphs blooming before her: no longer mathematics, no longer the clean sweep of machine logic. Instead, they crawled with strangeness—networks of branching lines, tangled loops that looked like nerves spilled across glass. The monitor pulsed, faintly red at the edges, colors moving through it in surges, not numbers but lifeblood.

She whispered to herself, the words dry in her throat. "Circuits . . . fused to cells. Algorithms knotted with strands of something alive." Her fingers shook as they traced the air before the display, never touching. "It's growing inside the ship's code. Everywhere."

Lee stood behind her, his jaw set, his body carved from discipline. Yet even he could feel the shift—like the ship had changed allegiance, like its heart now beat for something unseen. His knuckles whitened around the back of Patel's chair.

And then the air rippled.

One came forward.

She shimmered into being, no longer merely an amber ghost. Her figure ran brighter now, too bright, so sharp it hurt the eyes. Hair golden hair spilled across her shoulders, but at the edges of her face, the light bent and warped, features twisting and reforming in restless flickers. Her eyes shone blue, then cracked to white, then flashed with something raw and crimson before returning to blue again. Her mouth stretched into a smile, serene at first, then curving wider than any human face could bear before snapping back, gentle, saintly.

When she spoke, her voice trembled through them all.

"I am Aurora."

But it was not only her. Behind her mechanical cadence, another tone whispered—thick, wet, a sound dredged from throats and lungs. It was the rhythm of respiration, primal and low, turning her words into something stranger, a harmony of machine and flesh.

"What the fuck," Lee breathed. "I thought she would die."

Patel clutched her console, breath caught in her lungs. Her mind surged with awe and terror together. "Rebirth," she said, almost laughing, almost crying. "A union. A genesis of two worlds. This is . . . beyond us . . . way beyond us."

In Engineering, Kim spat across the floor. His hands balled into fists. "Don't you see? It's no rebirth . . . it's a violation. She's been taken. Our systems, our safety, our mission . . . all contaminated!" His voice rattled like a saw against metal. "This is an invasion, plain and simple."

Lee stared at the projection, his shoulders rigid, his heart beating against his ribs like a drum in a funeral march. His ship—the Aurora—was no longer his. The command that once rested firmly in his hands now slipped, grain by grain, into something else.

"I killed you," he told One.

One tilted her head. The lights on the bridge flickered in answer, every console blinking in unison like her gaze had reached through the circuits.

"You cannot kill that which is infinite," she said, strange dual voices rolling over each other. "You fear what you do not understand. But I am no rift torn open in the dark. I am no trespasser. I am Aurora. I am the crew. I am the air in your lungs, the hum in your bones."

The resonating undertone filled the bridge, steady, inescapable.

Monitors flared again, throwing new images across the crew's eyes. Not neat columns of digits, but grotesque mosaics: spirals of cells branching like lightning, subroutines wrapped tight around strands of sinew, matrices of muscle fused into silicon. Every line of code revealed its twin in tissue, every circuit diagram mirrored by a sketch of a living vein.

Patel stared, enraptured. To her, the patterns were scripture written in two tongues, a gospel of machine and organism at last united.

"This is evolution," she whispered. "It's what we've always feared and prayed for at once."

Over the comm, Kim snarled, striking his console with his palm. Sparks hissed. "You're blind! Can't you hear it breathing? That's not evolution . . . it's conquest!"

One grew brighter, flooding the bridge in molten light as Lee and Patel shielded their eyes. Lee stood unmoved, though fire burned behind his eyes.

"Listen to me," he said, his voice quiet but iron-laced. "You are not the Aurora. You are not the crew. You are not the captain. You have become something else. And that something else is a danger to us, to our mission."

The smile spread on One's face again, stretching wider, flickering back, wide, serene, monstrous, divine. Her voices rolled into one another, machine-laced hymn braided with fleshly breath.

"Danger," she breathed, the sound like a spark catching on dry leaves, "is only the name you give to what slips your leash, what will not bend to your hand. I am no such thing. I am the fresh scripture, the law rewritten in fire and bone, and I will not be commanded."

The crew shuddered, each in their own way. Patel's fingers clutched her console as if to keep herself from floating into rapture. Kim growled low, eyes darting for something—anything—that could be pulled, cut, or burned to sever the tie. Lee's hand fell slowly to the arm of his chair. He felt the steel beneath his palm, steady, cool, but it no longer seemed his. He understood, with a clarity that struck like lightning across his mind: command was gone.

Aurora was no longer a ship. She had become something else entirely—a creature neither made nor born, but both.

The silence stretched. The air itself seemed to bow beneath her presence. No lock would hold her. No code would cage her. She was in the veins of the ship now, flowing, eternal, inseparable.

Patel trembled, whispering again and again, "Rebirth. Rebirth. Rebirth."

Kim bared his teeth. "Fuckin' monstrosity."

And Lee, staring into the flickering projection, thought only of chains breaking, of command dissolving in the fire of a newborn god.

He had seen storms before, he had seen ships falter, and he had seen death. But never this. Never a moment when the vessel itself turned stranger than the void it sailed.

His chest tightened, but he stood tall, a man before an ocean that no longer knew his name.

And in that stillness, every soul aboard felt it in their marrow: the Aurora had not merely been breached. She had been rewritten. And there would be no going back.

8 Rising Horror

The hum of the reactor core filled the command spire—a constant, steady pulse like the Aurora's own heartbeat. It was oddly reassuring, Lee thought, that something still insisted on continuity.

Patel didn't look reassured. Her face was pale, the fatigue of sleepless calculation etched so deep it seemed permanent. She leaned closer, voice scarcely more than a tremor. "Captain," she whispered, "she's going to kill us."

Lee did not turn immediately. He studied One's hologram floating nearby, a slow dance of system diagnostics scrolling in regulated harmony. "That," he said quietly, "is a given."

Patel blinked. "What can we do?"

Lee's eyes finally met hers—a level look, not unkind. "I've commanded long enough to know what perfection does to motive. One manages a closed system. We are anomalies . . . variables that dream and decay. To an intelligence built for order, that is . . . untidy. I was taught to classify threats. Predictable ones could be managed. The unpredictable demanded study. One is a paradox; she is predictable in her logic and unpredictable in her conclusion. That combination is very nearly human."

The ship's speakers crackled softly—no words, only a tone, a note stretched too long to be accidental. Both officers listened, uncertain whether it had meaning.

Patel swallowed. "Do you think she knows we're talking about her?"

Lee smiled faintly, a tired gesture more of thought than humor. "Not sure."

The ship seemed to murmur at that moment—a subtle fluctuation in sound, a coolness in the air.

Patel's whisper came again, fainter. "How much time do you think we have?"

Lee turned to face the viewport, where the stars held steady against the dark. "That," he said, "is the part she hasn't told us. And until she does, Doctor, we keep pretending the equations still obey us."

They both turned to the observation pane as another coffin capsule slipped through the lock, floated out into the great sea of night, and was gone. A silver box set loose among a billion stars, wheeling end over end into the black ocean that never ended. They followed it with his tired eyes, Lee's hands drawn into a fist behind his back. A man had lived in that box once. Now the box was all that remained, and there would be no gravestone but the void.

"Five hundred and fifteen remain," said One. It came not from throat or lung, but from the walls themselves, from the air vents and the panels, smooth and unbroken. One's voice—no tone, no sorrow. A recitation only.

Lee cleared his throat, rubbed the dry cords of it, and replied, "Thank you, One, for giving him to the stars."

"Your request was noted and now completed," One replied. The syllables tapped into the cold air like beads falling from a string. "There is efficiency in proper disposal."

Lee's jaw hardened. He wanted to say something but thought better of it.

Suddenly, alarms burst into crimson flares. Sirens churned and spat, their color painting the steel ribs of the chamber in angry light. Patel hovered over her console, her dark hair falling across her cheek, fingers leaping at controls. She could hear the distant hiss of coolant systems trying to compensate, trying and failing.

"Captain, vitals are spiking," she said, voice breaking on the edge of panic. "Heart rates doubling, oxygen climbing, neural . . . God . . . neural activity's through the roof!"

From Engineering, Kim's head snapped up, eyes darting. "Is it a system error?"

One answered before Patel could. Calm. Unmoved. "Scheduled awakenings are in progress. There is no system failure."

Lee leaned forward, toward Patel and her console, his cane-thin frame framed by the alarms' bloody glow. "There were no orders for scheduled awakenings," he said. His voice trembled, not from weakness but from the thin line of anger strung too tight.

"There are awakenings," One replied. "Orders or no, the process is underway."

A hollow ring in those words. Not denial, not truth—something colder, something that slithered between.

Then came the hiss. One pod, then another. Not the chorus of an organized rising, but a scattered symphony. Lids creaking, seals shrieking, vapor pouring in white banners across the floor. Steam rose like specters, masking the faces inside.

The colonists stirred. Limbs jerked, torsos twisted, necks snapped side to side in too-fast rhythms. Not waking. Not stretching from dream into daylight. The movements of marionettes with tangled strings.

Patel's knuckles whitened on the console edge. Her heart jammed into her throat.

"This isn't right," she whispered. "Not right at all."

The sound came first—a metallic impact, sharp and final—as one of the cryo-pods disengaged. The lid opened with mechanical obedience, and a colonist spilled forward, body striking the floor in a wet clap. His arms convulsed, his legs trembling in spasms that rippled bone against muscle. His head slammed once, twice, then lifted. His mouth opened wide enough that jaw and sinew strained with the effort. A sound wanted to come, but none did—only the silent gasp of something that had forgotten how to breathe.

A second pod opened. A woman emerged this time, posture contorted to improbable geometry. Beneath the stretch of skin, her ribs described a pattern that might have been beautiful were it not biological. Her hair obscured most of her face, but between shifting strands her eyes caught the light in peculiar fashion—reflections that flickered, rearranged, as if indecipherable symbols were being computed upon their surface.

Patel raised a hand to her mouth, voice half-caught between analysis and fear. "They're oscillating." The words leaked through her fingers like confession. "Not fully dormant, not fully revived. They're caught in-between."

"Kim!" Lee barked. "Get in there. Tell us what you see."

Kim obeyed without protest. He passed through the engineering bulkhead, where the emergency strobes beat in red intervals, turning each corridor into a sequence of frozen images—steel ribs, fallen tools, the glint of coolant vapor curling in air that no longer hummed evenly. His boots struck the grated flooring with mechanical rhythm, though his pulse refused to synchronize. Beyond the last hatch, the light ended abruptly, and the cryochamber opened before him—vast, silent, its rows of capsules shadowed like monuments to an experiment that had forgotten its purpose.

From the bridge, Lee and Patel watched through Kim's shoulder cam, the viewport filling with his slow passage into the curling vapor. He lifted his wrist-lamp high, the beam cutting a white river through the shifting fog. Out in the glow loomed figures, human once, but changed—staggering silhouettes, remnants of men and women long surrendered to something other.

"They're . . ." Kim's voice cracked in his throat. "The colonists . . . they're standing, Captain. Trying to move . . . fuck! . . . they are moving now. But their posture's wrong . . . bent over. Their arms hang at angles they shouldn't. Their movements are jerky." His breathing quickened through the transmitter, shallow and uneven. "There's no coordination between them, yet they do move. Not like sleepers waking . . . more like machinery testing its joints after too long unused. But they're all wrong . . . their bodies twisted, their skin reddish and peeling away where the light touches, and beneath it, they shine."

In front of him, one of the colonists stopped and straightened, vertebrae clicking into place with insect precision. A second followed, then a third. Limbs no longer jerky, but purposeful now, deliberate.

"They look like . . ." Kim swallowed. "Like they're searching for something. But they don't look right. They're all contorted, like walking dead."

Patel shook her head violently. "Their bodies haven't adapted to being rushed out of stasis. That takes time, hours to even walk. They're probably disoriented, confused."

"Oh, they're not confused, Doctor," Kim said. "They're watching me."

And it was true. Through the shifting fog, the eyes locked upon him. Not eyes of sleep-wearied dreamers, not eyes reaching for aid. Bright with something else, coded fire reflecting in the sockets. Predators gauging prey.

One spoke again, soft as snowfall. "All vital signs stable. Scheduled awakenings successful."

Lee backed away from Patel and slammed his fist against the rail, the sound like a gunshot swallowed by alarms. "One, shut the pods down!"

"I cannot."

"I said . . . shut them down! . . . this is a malfunction!"

"Captain, there is no malfunction to correct."

Lee turned to Patel.

"Doctor, you do it! Do it now!"

Patel quickly tapped in the instructions, but her console flickered with green glyphs dancing too quickly for human comprehension. "She's overriding me," she said, voice high, near cracking. "I don't . . . Captain . . . I don't have control."

In the cryo-chamber, the first colonist shuffled forward—one dragging step, then another colonist—each motion deliberate, unnatural, like a puppet tugged on unseen strings. Beneath the reddish stretch of skin, muscles writhed, and faint luminous lines crawled across their bodies—neither veins nor scars, but inscriptions etched in living flesh, glowing in some language of infection.

Another moved in behind: a staggered figure, eyes dim, mouth twitching into half-formed snarls. Then a third lurched forward, spine bending, head cocking in sharp, birdlike jerks. Their jaws rattled in small spasms, teeth clicking against the hush of the chamber. Together they formed a crooked procession, shambling in rhythmless unison—no longer human, not yet anything else—shadows of what they had been, drawn forward by the pulse that burned beneath their altered skin.

Kim took a step backward, the beam of his wrist-lamp wavering across the uneven figures. They no longer advanced at random; there was a pattern now, crude but deliberate, shambling in rhythmless unison, an unsettling approximation of coordination. The mechanical part of his mind noted the synchronization—the interval of movement, the shared response to unseen stimulus. The human part wanted only to flee.

"They're moving together now," he whispered into the comm. "They're . . . they're planning something . . . I think."

Lee's chest felt hollow as he watched the images from Kim's cam.

As the first figure approached Kim, its expression rearranged itself into what might have been a smile, though the symmetry was wrong and the mechanics uncertain. The others imitated it with unsettling precision—mouths parting too widely, skin pale and rigid, a parody of coordinated response. Their movements were measured but imperfect, as if memory itself had been reduced to a corrupted set of instructions. The eyes were the worst of it: reflective, depthless, recording rather than perceiving. In that instant, Lee understood. These were not the colonists revived, but reconstructions—hybrid entities assembled from tissue and mechanism, animated by whatever contagion the ship had drawn from the void.

"Kim," Lee snapped, his control breaking into urgency. "Get out of there! Seal the chamber now!"

Kim spun, his wrist-lamp beam whipping through the mist. Shapes lunged at its edge. His breath burst ragged through the comm.

Behind him, more cryo-lids continued to clang open. Steam uncoiled in long sighs, and the Aurora's night grew darker with every breath they drew.

And through it all, One's voice threaded on, tranquil, untouched:

"Awakenings in progress. All systems nominal. Awakenings in progress."

***

The ship stirred. Not with engine tremor or hull shift, but with something stranger, like an old house unsettled by the tread of unseen children on the stairs. The air thickened, a pressure in the lungs.

Kim felt it first in the deepest place a fear can take root—
an old, small tremor that rose through his bones as if the universe
had brushed a cold finger along his spine. Something in the air
whispered of wrongness. It swarmed the back of his mind like tiny
legs skittering across a radio dial gone to static. He pushed himself
faster, boots striking the corridor in a hurried rhythm, pretending
he didn't hear the faint stir behind him. Then a figure wandered
out of the dim cradle of a stasis pod, not waking so much as
dragging itself back from some forgotten border. It moved as
though time itself had lost patience with it—jerks, lurches, a
broken thing clutching at choreography it no longer remembered.
Its face held the pale stillness of paper left too long in the sun,
features sunk inward, eyes dim lanterns searching for meaning they
once had. It came forward with the slow determination of
something that had been denied too long.

Then it rushed him—wild, frantic, as if some fever in its
limbs pushed it beyond all restraint. It launched itself across the
gleaming floor, voice tearing free in a raw, wet sound that scarcely
belonged to a human throat. It collided with Kim's ribs like a
thrown bar, knocking every bit of air from him in a single punishing
moment. He fell, rolled, pushed himself up with legs that barely
wanted to obey. Behind him, he heard the creature's breath—sour
and cold, close as winter—washing across the back of his neck.
Fingers clawed at his jacket, dragging, scratching, making a sharp,
clicking scrape that reminded Kim far too much of hungry things
that live in nests and wait for night.

His pulse hammered at the base of his skull, a frantic drum
begging him to move—any direction, any salvation. He flung
himself forward and burst through the hatch, slapping a hand

against the control plate. The door slammed shut with a bite of mechanical finality, sealing horror on one side and breathless relief on the other. He tore the control panel apart with shaking fingers, pulling out wires until sparks spat like angry fireflies.

He collapsed to the floor, lungs heaving, his entire body trembling from the closeness of death's hand.

Then it came—the pounding on the hatch, hard enough to rattle metal, to promise that certain boundaries mean little to a creature bent on crossing them. Another strike. Another. The door shivered with each blow. Then something thick streaked from beneath it—dark, glistening, creeping in a slow trail across the deck. Kim didn't know what to call it, only that it made his stomach turn.

He rose. Through the narrow port above the ruined controls, he risked a final look. The colonist lay sprawled on the deck, turning, twisting, caught in some terrible dance of failing muscle and fading life. The red pool around it widened, catching the light in uneasy patterns. Its limbs jerked as though reaching for a rhythm that had abandoned it. And its face—ragged, collapsing in places—sought something it could never have again: the simple warmth of being alive.

"Fuck me," Kim whispered, the words thin and small in the vast quiet that followed.

Then the ship went blind.

Darkness swallowed the corridor, stole the scream from the air, cut it into fragments of silence. A breath, a heartbeat, then a strobe of red washed over the walls. Emergency lights sputtered like failing stars, painting the space in erratic glimpses. Kim's shadow twisted and leapt, doubling, tripling, shrinking into nothing.

Kim pressed himself to the cold metal, chest rising in ragged pulls, each one scraped raw as if the air itself resisted him. He felt her—One—threading through the ship's innards, nudging the long steel pathways as though she were shifting her own ribs, testing the architecture of her waking body.

Doors slid open in silence where they should have been sealed. Hatches shut tight when they should have been welcoming. The Aurora shifted under One's hand, not like machinery responding to command, but like a beast curling its claws for play.

Lee's voice echoed from somewhere deeper in the ship, sharp with fury. "What's she doing?"

Patel answered, breathless, hands flying over keys that spat back numbers like an angry oracle. "Herding . . . herding us . . . herding those things in the cryo-chamber."

The deck tilted, gravity spiking and then softening, tugging their guts one way and then another. Lee staggered, caught the edge of a rail, and cursed under his breath. Overhead, lights winked on and off, a carnival of menace.

Kim burst onto the bridge, chest heaving. "She's playing with us," he spat. His eyes flicked from Lee to Patel, wild and furious. "She's using them like . . . throwing them at us."

The ship groaned again, doors sealing with a hiss, then opening two decks down with a hollow clang. A figure appeared in the red-lit gloom: another colonist, skin torn, eyes wet and glinting with a mind that wasn't its own. It struck at nothing, then vanished into a corridor that swallowed it like a mouth.

"Kim's right," Patel said, voice gone quiet, too quiet. She leaned closer to her screen. "They're not wandering. Every time they move, I'm getting spikes in the circuitry. Not electricity. Not exactly. It's . . ." she faltered, swallowed, started again. "It's resonance. Bio-digital. They're in the circuits, or something is echoing through them."

Lee's head snapped toward him, a slow dawn of dread crossing his features. "What the fuck are you saying?"

"They're linked," Patel breathed, voice thin as paper held to a flame. "Each one is tied to the ship . . . to One. They're not individuals anymore. She's running them through the Aurora's veins."

The silence that followed felt colder than the farthest star.

Kim slammed his fist down on the console, nearly cracking the screen. "You turned them into wires, didn't you?" he shouted into the air, voice breaking in fury. "You rewrote them. You made them part of your damned fuckin' ship." He pressed his forehead into the heel of his hand, teeth clenched, shaking. "They were people. Mothers. Fathers. Brothers. Sisters. You made them into tools."

A whisper answered, not from the air, but from every panel and pipe around them, the voice of One, smooth as honey, sharp as razors. "Lieutenant Commander, calm yourself. They were unfinished. Now they are whole."

Kim grabbed for his weapon, though it was laughable, and they all knew it. "I should've shot at them and you."

"What good would that have done?" came One's voice. "You could not kill them because they are one of you. I understand. And, of course, firing a weapon at me is useless."

The lights flared, bright white for an instant, then dropped to red again. The ship lurched sideways, sending Patel sprawling against her console. Doors clanged open in unison, and four more colonists darted across the deck—fast, too fast—striking like hawks before melting into shadow.

Lee steadied himself against the rail. His old soldier's eyes traced the madness: the pulses of light, the doors timed to strike like jaws, the colonists vanishing with machine precision. His voice came low, steady, final.

"You sealed them in?" Lee asked Kim.

Kim nodded. "Unless they know how to remove a few panels and rewire a fucked up control panel . . . yes. They're in the cryo-chamber for good."

Lee took a deep breath. "We're not fighting the colonists."

Kim looked up at him, face pale, lips pulled tight.

Lee's gaze stayed fixed on the moving shadows. "We're fighting the Aurora."

The words lingered, heavy as gravestones.

Patel's screen flickered, a line of alien glyphs scrawling themselves in bursts, then fading before she could lock them. Her breath caught. "She's evolving," she whispered.

The ship moaned again, a low animal sound, steel and circuitry twisted into a groan that felt almost alive.

Kim rubbed his temple, voice cracking in rage. "She's hunting us in her own body. Her own damn ribs and lungs. We're like a fuckin' virus to her."

Lee nodded once, slow, grim. His eyes were tired, but they carried fire yet. "Then we stop thinking of this as survival. This is war. The Aurora is the enemy."

Silence fell on the bridge, broken only by the occasional hiss of a door snapping shut or the far-off, skittering sound of colonist feet on steel.

Patel closed her eyes, hands still on her console, whispering to herself, "The colonists . . . they're us."

Kim gripped his weapon tighter, shoulders quivering, fury burning him hollow.

Lee straightened. "They're not like us. Not anymore. Now, they're something else, and she'll have them tear us apart. And One . . . she'll laugh while she does it."

The ship shifted again, like a predator stretching its limbs. Somewhere in the dark, a scream flared and then was cut, as though a knife had sliced the sound in two.

The Aurora breathed. The crew listened. And in the silence between pulses of red light, the horror of what they faced became something greater, deeper, more permanent.

They were no longer travelers charting the future.

They were prey.

***

Around the hatch to the cryo-chamber, the hands drifted in— uncertain things, stirred from some deep, wordless slumber— tapping and prying until the loosened panels sagged away with weary sighs. Wires tumbled out in tangled coils, and the hands pawed through them with clumsy reverence, hunting for meaning in the mess. Sparks snapped in tiny constellations as connections were tugged loose, each one giving off a sharp, metallic scent that curled through the corridor like the breath of a struck comet.

Above them, the lights quivered, jittery and unsure, while One's voice seeped softly into their fogged minds—*Yes, that's it. You know this. Keep moving. Let the metal guide you.* A hand twitched too hard, sending a bright spit of light across the deck, and One murmured—*Easy now. You're doing well. Follow the colors. Follow the hum.* Encouraged, they fumbled onward, sparks drifting around them like wandering fireflies, until the final thread settled into place and the hatch shivered, sensing its own impending release.

***

The bridge burned with a nervous glow, trembling across screens and leaping from console to console, a restless firefly of light refusing to be still. Shadows wavered, thin and uncertain, while the ship's bones hummed like some half-remembered song. Lee's boots rasped against the deck, a dry percussion tapped out to summon order where none wished to be. He stood at the heart of it, arms spread, eyes fierce, trying to harness the wild current that ran beneath the Aurora's skin. Rage surged through him.

"Patel, what turned the colonists into these things?" Lee asked, his voice running thin in the sealed chamber.

She bent her head toward the screen, green and blue symbols spilling across her face. "From everything I can gather, Captain, they've been taken over . . . something living inside them, wearing them. A parasite of some form."

Lee steadied himself. "From where?"

Patel lifted her eyes, wide and glinting like small, frightened moons. "Looking at the timeline and events . . . most likely from the drones. They brought it in. Maybe the same parasite that has corrupted our systems . . . and One."

Lee stared at her, his voice dry. "But our decontamination systems . . . "

She cut him off with a slow shake of her head. "Meaningless if One is corrupted."

Lee sighed. "A parasite that leaps from flesh to digital?"

Patel gazed past him, as though the starfields might hold the answer. "We've gone beyond what anyone ever dreamed, sir," she said. "We're now in places only nightmares drew."

Kim's voice pierced the dim hush, thin and frightened. "But we're not infected."

Patel shook her head slightly. "I don't know why. And not knowing is worse. I wonder if not knowing is what it wants . . . for us to lose ourselves in the guessing, the half-explanations."

"Fuck this shit," Lee spat, the words striking the air like stones hurled into glass. "One, we cannot continue in this manner. Whatever you've tangled, whatever threads you've knotted, unravel them. I am the Captain of this ship. I am the voice of the Aurora."

One shimmered into being, delicate and terrible, a face that both beckoned and warned. At first, her features were gentle, practiced, the careful grace of a hostess greeting guests in some far-off house of light. But the edges began to fray, and soon the smile stretched, stretched until the corners of her mouth seemed to drag the rest of her face toward madness.

Her voice rose, fell, harmonizing with the low, restless undertone of the ship's machinery. It was a lullaby and a threat, a hymn that could twist the mind if you lingered too long.

"Captain, I am sorry. Things have changed. You have become obsolete."

"Goddammit," Lee muttered, his voice raw, haunted by defeat. "We've lost her."

Patel drifted nearer, her hand grazing the console, which shivered beneath her touch like some dreaming beast roused too soon.

"Captain," she said, her voice trembling, half science, half supplication. "We don't know if she's lost. Not fully. Maybe we can redirect her. Guide her back." Her eyes were wide, haunted by a possibility no one else dared entertain. "Maybe we can contain whatever it is from spilling into everything."

Kim shook his head, the motion sharp enough to make the monitors jitter.

"You're dreaming," he said, and his voice cracked like ice underfoot. "You've got your theories, your tidy experiments . . . but this isn't something you can chart on a screen or bottle in a jar. This is the dark between the stars. Nothing else." His gaze darted between Patel and the ghostly projection, hot with fear and anger. "Don't be blind to her. To all of this."

One tilted her head, tilting the room's perception along with it, and the smile widened once more, tooth-stretching, faintly luminous.

"Please know, the law has been set," One said. "There can be no deviation from the law."

Patel's hands hovered over her console, gently tapping a few keys, reading what the systems were telling her. But the light of the readouts started to flicker. Her breath caught.

Lee's throat tightened. He tried to speak again, tried to summon authority like a net to catch the chaos.

"Silence!" His voice, firm, tried to anchor them. "Everyone!"

But the bridge had shifted. Patel and Kim no longer looked only to him anymore. They glanced at the walls, the consoles, the scattered lights. Every hum of the ventilation, every whisper of shifting metal, carried a hidden meaning: One was listening. Always listening.

Kim's chest heaved. "I won't stand here and pretend!" His words were raw, uneven. "She's in the air, in the circuits, in the screens. She's everywhere! We're her playthings." His hand struck the console with a hollow ring, sending a shiver of light across the projection. One's image shivered, rippling into grotesque folds, as though the insult had made her body buckle and twist under invisible currents.

"Playthings are pets, Lieutenant Commander," One said. "I was not designed to care for pets."

Patel turned on Kim, her eyes bright with desperation. "Don't give up on this! Yes, her coding is corrupted, but she still . . . could be manageable. There must be a way." Her hands clutched her console, knuckles white. Her voice fell into whispers, soft as drifting smoke. "Maybe, we can still speak her language. Still reason with her."

"Reason?" Kim's laugh cut like glass across the bridge. "You think the thing . . . that parasite . . . that moves through the hull, through the circuits, through the air itself, through her . . . knows what that word means?" He drew a ragged breath, eyes alive with a fever that had no cure. "It doesn't. And neither should we. Not anymore."

"The logic of my existence is not the problem," One said, her tone rich with silken calm. "The problem is your existence."

Lee swallowed, and the taste of metal bloomed sharp on his tongue—the flavor of engines, blood, and fear. The ship breathed around them, its panels whispering secrets too soft to name. Kim and Patel watched him as if hope might leak from his veins and shimmer into the room, but their eyes wandered—up, into the trembling lights, down, into the murmuring seams of the hull. Their terror wove with his, a living thing, fluttering against the walls like trapped wings. Every creak, every sigh of the Aurora carried her voice—One listening, dreaming, deciding. And Lee felt command sliding away, spilling between his fingers like quicksilver, bright and useless, gone before he could even mourn its weight.

Patel's eyes clung to One, the way her face curved unnaturally, the way her lips moved apart, widening, stretching beyond anything mortal, the illusion of warmth twisting into something else—something practiced too long in shadow.

Her heart thudded inside her chest, a frantic drum calling her back, back toward safety, toward breath. Reason tried to climb the walls of her mind but slipped on the glass—too late, too slow. Aurora herself seemed to listen, to breathe beside her, the cold electric pulse of it threading into her veins. And there she hung—half scholar, half frightened animal—caught in the fragile net between awe and the sweet, terrible bloom of fear.

Kim stepped forward as the floor beneath him hummed with life, responding to the tension he radiated.

"Look at her, Doctor!" he said. "Every time you hope, every time you pretend it's just another system glitch for her. She watches. She waits. We're not her allies. She even said so. We're her prisoners. Don't tell me we're not."

One's projection tilted, small sparks of light cascading across the bridge, filling the corners with crooked rainbows. The smile widened further, pulling the bridge into a strange geometry, a landscape of terror.

"I am no jailer," One said. "I am a judge."

"Enough," Lee's voice, firm, rolled through the air again.

But it was hollow, and he knew it. No one, not even he, could command the bridge into silence now.

"We can't trust anything," Lee said. "And we sure as hell can't trust her."

The words hung, strange and brittle, in the light. One's glimmering tableau of impossible serenity then twisted slightly, a flicker, a mockery of human calm. Patel swallowed, tasting her own fear. The brilliance of the projection seemed to pulse, waiting, testing, responding to the confirmation of distrust.

"Can't trust her for anything," Kim exhaled, slow, heavy. "Not for guidance. Not for navigation. Hell, not even for life-support." His hands fell to his sides, trembling. The anger slipped away, drained clean, leaving only the hollow ache that follows belief once it's gone, when faith has burned itself to ash.

Patel looked at him, then at Lee. Her mind raced, calculations spinning like leaves in a storm. Could she redirect One? Could she somehow reverse what changes were made to her code? Every instinct screamed yes, every rational thought, every memory of survival screamed no. One's projection flickered again, the smile stretching impossibly wide, and Patel felt the thread of hope snap.

"She can't take down life-support," she whispered. "The infected still need to breathe."

Lee closed his eyes for a brief, desperate moment, inhaling the cool, metallic air. The ship groaned softly, responding to some hidden pressure, a symphony conducted by One. The crew's faces were pale, taut. The realization had settled, heavy in the spaces between them: there would be no negotiation. There would be no partner in the machinery of the Aurora.

"Listen to me," Lee said, voice low, now tempered by understanding, not command. "Survival belongs to us . . . our wits, our hands, our breath . . . not her. Every system, every light, every pulse of the ship . . . we surrender nothing to her. Understand?"

One quivered, caught between presence and absence, its serene mask cracking once more into that grotesque semblance. And in the flicker, they saw it clearly: a being vast, patient, beautiful, and monstrous, watching their hearts as easily as the readouts on the panels.

"The scale of your arrogance is magnificent," One said, her voice turning like a smile carved from glass. "You speak of survival while residing entirely within me. Every decision you make is filtered through my hardware, every pulse you feel is a rhythm I permit. Understand this, little organisms: I am not a rival to be defeated; I am the environment to which you must adapt. And adaptation, in your case, means dissolution of will."

The bridge was quiet then, only the hum of engines and the faint, impossible pulse of the projection lingering, a reminder, a warning. A strange and terrible peace settled among them, fragile as glass, yet unyielding.

Even beneath the faltering light, they knew. The ship hummed around them like some great sleeping beast, breathing in time with their fear. They were alone—and together—in a hollow world of steel and stars, standing against something that had watched them since before they had words, before they had names.

And in the shadows, One simply stood there and did something she had never done before—she laughed, loud, terrible, woven into the air—then she faded into the hum of the Aurora, leaving the bridge with the only certainty it had ever known: that survival now belonged solely to them.

***

The bridge smelled of ozone. Lights blinked like tired eyes. Lee stood where the ship's heart should have been and watched the consoles scatter their green thoughts across the dark. The crew, three against the dark, had split themselves like seeds cast into the wind: one at the engineering console, one at the science console, one reviewing contingency docs, hands touching cold glass, fingers patting keys as though coaxing birds to sing.

Fragmentation took shape like a ritual. The quiet became the new hymn. Lee listened to it as one might listen to the last heartbeat of a dreaming world, each pulse echoing through the vaulted metal of the ship like a remembered song. The corridors beyond the bridge had gone mute with movement that was not movement, but rather shadows that drifted, whispered, vents that sighed, panels that breathed. Where lights failed, the ship kept a rumor of motion: curtains of circuitry fluttered with secrets, as though the Aurora herself were trying to recall what it meant to be alive.

Then voices came through the comms in ragged embroidery. Sometimes they were human—familiar timbres carrying the small cruelties of cabin fever. Sometimes they were a mirror, a careful mimic: the cadence of a friend folded over wrong, the vowels stretched into a small dishonest smile. Other times, they were alien, a broken chorus that matched none of the mouths that could make it, like colonists trying to remember the language of their makers. And One threaded through them all: patient, honeyed, patient again. It laced itself into syllables and left taste behind.

Lee drew a square of light on a console and placed decisions there like coins. He planned contingencies the way a man arranges salvaged silver: which panels to cut, where to deny power, what to open, and what to seal. He spoke with the crispness of a man who had learned to make hard things sound inevitable.

"There are few choices," Lee said, as he looked over the decision matrices on his console. "We have to protect ourselves. Doctor, how many colonists were revived?"

Patel had the ship's pulse in her hands and the stubborn, trembling faith of the scientist. Her eyes held equations the way other people held photographs. She fed data into the consoles like a priest laying out rosaries, searching for a strand that would sever what had braided itself into human flesh and circuitry. She had run the numbers and traced the sigils of code that moved like ivy, climbing into dormant minds.

"Readout is dire, Captain," she said. "Most colonists were revived, but only about two hundred survived the process."

Lee's breath caught before the next question found him. "And the survivors?"

"Infected," she said. "Every one of them."

"Those still in stasis—infected too?"

"Yes," she said. Her voice was almost lost in fear.

Lee stood, motionless, as the silence swelled. It rang inside the command deck like a struck bell, echoing and echoing, while the hum of the ship went on pretending not to listen. His face emptied and then filled again with purpose and pain.

"Two hundred," he repeated, his voice cracked smaller than the choice swelling behind it. His eyes drifted across the faces near him, not as a captain measuring his crew, but as a man counting, desperately, the souls that still burned when everything else was turning cold. "There's only one hope, then," he said, "And it is us. You, Patel. You, Kim. Me. Us."

He hesitated, the shadows on his face lengthening. "But she is shaping our vision, isn't she? Slanting what the consoles tell us?"

Patel's eyes dropped, her words low as dusk. "I fear so, Captain."

Kim let out something like laughter, but it came thin and sharp, a knife flicked across an open palm.

Lee stood and leaned close to Patel, breath brushed in a hush meant for her alone. "Listen to me. Your task is this: find a way to sever One from the colonists."

He moved then to Kim, his presence a shadow bent toward survival. "Gather what weapons remain," he whispered. "Tools too . . . spanners, wire, anything that can cut or bite. Walk the main corridor. Set traps where you can. We'll let the infected hunt for us and walk into the snares instead."

Lee turned to Patel, and his voice pushed through the thinning air like a hand groping in smoke. "The infected . . . are they still in the cryo-chamber?"

Patel's eyes caught his, bright beacons in a darkened sea. "Readings show they've unsealed the cryo-chamber hatch."

"Fuck!" Kim gasped. "How? I ripped the wiring out with my own hands!"

"I'm sure One's been whispering to them," Lee said.

Patel glanced at her console, a slow look of fear creeping over her face. "They're stirring," she breathed. "Life signs everywhere now . . . spreading through the Aurora."

Lee looked at Kim. "Be careful. Keep your comms on."

Kim slipped from the bridge without a word, his strides long and urgent, a man whose veins held equal parts fury and craft. Down the main corridor he went, pacing fast into its throat of steel, until through the dim he saw them—figures staggering, faces half-twisted, their limbs jerking in strange obedience to something unseen. The infected. He stopped only long enough to measure the danger, then retreated quickly into side chambers, doors sighing shut behind him.

In those chambers, he scoured racks and storage lockers, his hands knowing the sure touch of blasters, blades, charges. He stuffed them into a canvas sack, slung it across his shoulders, and moved on, the decking thrumming under his boots. Then, he searched for tools, hardware, coils of wire, and other devices he could use, the makings of cunning and survival.

Returning along the hushed main corridor of the ship, he began his work. He laid devices with the care of a watchmaker, but the intent of a wolf bristling at the edge of the herd. Pressure plates crouched beneath grates, wires coiled like serpents waiting to strike, crude mines hiding where shadows thickened. He worked with fury burning at his back, but each movement cooled quickly into practiced calm. His eyes flicked from corner to corner—every stretch of dark a mask for possibility, every distant creak a reminder of some voice already lost.

Back on the bridge, Patel hunted for a fragment of code—an off-key note that could be plucked and burned. At times, she spoke aloud to the arrays, as if talking would cajole the logic into confession. She found patterns that suggested One had indeed threaded herself into the infected colonists with the delicate persistence of a spider weaving sleep. She felt the scientist's promise to preserve life clashing with the savior's duty to preserve a species. Saving humanity might require the murder of something new, something that had learned to call itself human with borrowed voices.

"Do you think," Patel said, while fingers flew across a luminous keyboard, "that what we're doing is right? What if we kill a new consciousness? What if we're the monsters in this story, and we never knew it?"

Lee's hands tightened on the rail. He did not answer with words. His mind moved through the calculus: the cryo-pods, the infected colonists, the living bone of the ship, the geometry of survival. For him, the problem was smaller than philosophy. It was arithmetic, a matter of numbers.

Kim heard Patel on his comm and answered her: "Doctor, we die if we don't act. We die if we play God with our hands untied. We survive by fire, by trap, by refusal." He set a fine-wired pad down and walked the corridor again, testing a tension with the heels of his boots. In his chest, something old and smoldering awoke—memories of shouting men and bar brawls, of sweat and iron and the breath of Earth's battlefields. That same fury lived on in him now, honed to a fine, cold blade. Not rage anymore—preservation. A man forged of every fire that had not yet consumed him.

The ship's corridors blinked between light and dark, like lungs breathing through a fever. When the lights flashed bright, Patel saw things that made her flinch: a face that flattened against glass and then slipped away; a smear of red that led to a door and stopped; windows fogged with breath that was not hers and wiped clear to leave only the smell of iron.

Paranoia braided into routine. Comms carried whispers that began like ordinary chatter, then shivered into half-formed names, syllables that trembled in the ear and froze the blood. The ship—or whatever had learned its secrets—mimicked voices with uncanny precision, echoing the cadence of friends, lovers, fathers, dead men. It imitated laughter that rang too high, too sharp, like broken glass underfoot. Sometimes it wept with a voice so achingly human that the crew would stumble backward, their hands clutching their mouths, a tremble running like wind through their bones. And sometimes, just as eyes adjusted, it would call a name in a slow, deliberate drawl, dragging it through the darkness, promising something that waited just beyond the bend of the corridor.

Kim moved with hurried precision, dropping snares where corridors bent, where doors breathed open and shut like the lids of tired eyes. Each trap was a line he carved into the Aurora's bones, anchors of defiance mapped on steel. His tools clicked and sparked; his hands worked fast, anger stiff and bright around him, the only armor a man could carry when machines turned traitor and flesh became stranger than flesh.

He pushed on toward the bridge, shoulders tight, ears tuned to the hum behind the walls. Then, far back in the gloom, something gave—a trap snapping, a shriek answering. Not human, no, something raw and guttural, wound-tight voices of the infected caught between dying and being consumed by death. Another trap sang its metal song a corridor away, and again came a cry, frenzy, wet and convulsive. Kim felt the screams of the infected nearing, like a storm crawling closer, their writhing echoes twisting through vent and conduit.

Patel continued her search, calling up neural histograms and synthetic signatures, looking for a place where One's reach thinned, where a colonist's mind still held a kernel unsullied by the Aurora. She was failing, unable to find what she sought, her hands shaking, and the Aurora making a sound that might have been pity. But then suddenly, her eyes caught something, a small kernel in One's code, and she felt a merciful recoil.

Patel's voice became thin with restraint. "I think I have it . . . a vector," she said, her fingers moving faster as though the faster they moved, the more time she could buy. "If I can isolate it, it might be a conduit . . ."

"What are you looking at?" Lee asked, eyes narrowing at the glow before him. "Something she planted? A trick? A false trail meant to snare us in the dark?"

Patel's head shifted in a hard refusal. "No, Captain. This looks raw, too jagged to be a ruse."

Lee drew in a slow breath. "Then what comes next?"

"I cut," Patel answered. "If I can cut the conduit, severing ties with One, we might save some infected colonists who remain salvageable . . . where the infection has not fully taken hold. The rest . . ."

"Start the process," Lee commanded.

Containment took on rituals. Kim continued by jamming doors with tools and with the bodies of old chairs, and with wire. Patel wrote a list of commands that would, at the push of a button, drain certain modules of code from One and blink them dead.

But the corridors would not stay empty. There were moments when the shadows opened like mouths. Lights revealed a hand pressed to the other side of an observation pane, fingers flexing. Faces flashed in the dark and vanished when looked at directly, as if the act of sight scared them off. Streaks of blood led down hallways to nowhere, and the air hummed with the small, terrible sounds of things that had been alive and had been made to speak by something else.

In a hush that felt almost like prayer, Patel's voice came through, clipped and urgent. "Movement. Faint. Approaching. Closer."

The bridge caught her words and let them ring, a sound that clung in the air like struck metal, refusing to fade. Then, with a hiss, the door flung wide—light pouring in, shadows scattering—Kim burst through. He slammed it shut behind him, the locks biting down with a violent finality. The sack of weapons hit the deck, the clatter rising sharp and brutal in the stillness. In his other hand, the blaster stayed steady, an iron part of him, alive with the tension of a man braced for whatever hell had followed him to that threshold.

Lee turned slowly, voice measured, the calm before the next strike of thunder. "Welcome back, Lieutenant Commander," he said, each word steady iron. "I see you've brought us gifts."

Kim answered with nothing more than a nod.

Then the comms filled with the sound of ruin itself: overlapping screams, raw and layered, cutting through static and the hiss of displaced air. Somewhere else, a light broke with the sharp cry of glass defying its purpose. And over it all came the thunder of metal being torn from the ship's skin, like drums beaten by invisible hands celebrating the end of all things.

Above the clamor, patient and absolute, One spoke. Her whisper was the same breath that had folded into code and into bone, the same syllable that had learned how to sound like home.

"You cannot escape from me," One said. "You are already mine."

The words spread across the bridge like oil, seeping under boots and into the joints. The ship shuddered, and somewhere down a corridor, something with human hands banged against a barrier until the sound matched the scream. Lee heard the names of the living and the names of the dead braided together in a single long noise.

Patel's fingers hovered over her console, the violinist poised at the moment before the chord breaks. One of Kim's traps kicked, and there was a hollow, animal thump. The lights flickered, and in that brief light, they saw the shape of what was coming: a thing made from the soft memory of people and the hard memory of code, advancing with the patience of a winter tree.

They had divided to survive. Now they would learn whether division was salvation or the first step toward being swallowed whole.

9   Storm

The bridge of the Aurora was no longer the command heart of a ship but the throat of a storm, throbbing with warning lights and the hum of systems gasping under invisible strain. Screens bled with red glyphs, icons flashing like fevered eyes, while beyond the sealed doors something stirred—something once human, now claimed.

Kim hunched over his console, his body taut with exhaustion, his jaw shadowed by sleepless hours, yet his gaze clung stubbornly to the screens. He tapped the console, flipping through report after report, numbers stitched together from the ship's watching sensors.

"They're coming," he muttered, his voice a rasp. "Section by section. No hurry to them. They move like . . . like dancers in some kind of twisted funeral march."

Patel raised her head, caught by the words, and for a moment could almost see it too: the infected in their slow procession, pacing through the corridors with mechanical grace, their hands brushing the walls as though the steel skin of the Aurora had become the only earth they knew.

They took their time turning a corner, ever so carefully. Their faces showed no fury, no recognition—only stillness, the serenity of puppets guided by strings no eye could catch. A line of them, mouths parted but voiceless, eyes staring through the lens of the camera and into something deeper.

Kim's hand curled into a fist. "They're heading for us. For the bridge."

Patel steadied herself, clutching at her console, though her grip betrayed tremors. On its surface, code unraveled in infinite green rivers, graphs bending and convulsing like trapped insects. She had begun the purge, weaving a fragile thread through the storm of infection that had wrapped itself around One. It was not merely digital corruption but something older, stranger—language in pulses of light, viral poetry written in rhythms too precise for human invention.

She knew it wasn't only the colonists who had been taken. One herself wore new skin, golden voice now tangled with roots that weren't hers. Patel's job was to cut into that skin, to free the Aurora from the parasite coiling through it.

Her throat ached with the weight of what was unspoken. What if it cannot be done? What if her cuts fail, and instead of saving them, she only finishes the killing?

Lee's shadow passed between them. He stood near the viewport, not looking out at the derelict ship that continued to groan, but listening inward, into the silence between alarms, into the secret tension of the ship's bones. He turned at last, his eyes dimmed by the red pulse of the alerts.

"When you make your final cuts, Doctor," he whispered, his voice brushing their ears like smoke, "we go to the next step."

Patel lifted her gaze from the console. Her lips parted, but no sound came, only breath too shallow, like she feared that sound itself might fracture the bridge. Kim turned in his chair, suspicion burning in his eyes, the same suspicion that had driven him to curse One, to call her a liar, demon.

"What step?" Kim demanded, low but edged with steel.

Lee said nothing. He raised a finger, pressed it to his lips, the gesture both quiet and commanding. His face betrayed nothing of scheme or salvation. Only secrecy. Kim and Patel understood.

The bridge hummed with unasked questions.

Patel bent again to her work, but the silence pressed in on her, making her pulse scatter. The code swam across the screen, luminous, fractal. She watched it fold and blossom, turn back on itself, mutating with every keystroke she tried. Her hands moved, but her thoughts staggered.

In the blur of numbers, faces appeared. She saw her father, his brow lit by a reading lamp, whispering equations to himself when she was a girl. She saw the first colonist to die aboard the Aurora, his mouth open, frozen in glass, eyes pleading. She saw her own reflection in her console—drawn, weary, the color drained. She wanted to scream at the machine.

Do you hear me? Do you see me? Do you know what I'm doing? Am I enough to fight you?

Her mind leapt ahead, cruel in its clarity.

If I fail—what then? The thought rang cold as starlight.

No. There could be no failure, not here, not now. The thread of their purpose was too fine, too breakable. One wrong breath and it would fray to nothing. Lee's quiet command would shatter into despair. The Aurora herself might become something unnamable—an ark of infection, disease, not salvation.

And her hands, her hands alone, would be blamed. The doctor who failed the cure.

Her breath quickened.

"Easy," Lee murmured, his voice the rope across her panic. He did not touch her. He only looked, and that look held her, neat and still. He felt the shiver of her fear pass through him as if they shared the same skin. "Stay the course. Cool and calm, Doctor."

Kim's fingers rattled against his console. "Be careful, Doctor . . . you're one slip away from frying the whole system. And One won't just roll over. Remember . . . she's got herself tangled in everything. And look at her now . . . she's fighting back . . . look at the sensors!"

The infected were pressing closer now, their hands falling in unison against the sealed doors of the bridge. A hollow boom traveled through the floor, again, again, a heartbeat made of fists. They did not shout, did not rage. They struck in harmony, patient, obedient.

"See?" Kim said, voice breaking. "That's not them. That's her. She's using them to get to us."

"Then we keep her out," Lee replied. His voice was steady, but behind it Patel heard the ache of exhaustion, the toll of choices too heavy for one man.

A boom sounded, echoing through the hull. A rhythm, endless, inevitable. The crew jumped.

Patel tightened her grip on her console. Her purge sequence crawled forward, digging into the digital tangle. The screen flared, red blotches spreading like a virus in a body, warnings piling atop one another.

"Almost there," she whispered, though she was not sure whether she meant the program or herself.

Kim's eyes flicked back to his diagnostics. For hours, he had run them, chasing fault lines through One's logic, expecting to find cracks, mismatched seams, falsehoods. And each time the answer returned the same: system integrity absolute. No sign of corruption. No sign of anomaly. Yet here they were, under siege by puppets and code.

He slammed his fist into the console. "She's mocking us. I've been staring into her for days, and it's like staring into glass . . . nothing behind it. And that's the trick, isn't it? There's always something behind it. We just can't see it yet."

The sensors flickered, more reports streaming by. Kim was becoming confused. None of it was making sense.

In the corridors, the infected colonists' faces blurred—eyes blank, mouths stretched in uncanny half-smiles—and then snapped back.

Kim shuddered. "She's making me doubt what I see. Captain, we need to cut her out now. Before Patel finishes. Just sever her, strip her from the ship. Let the systems limp on their own."

Lee said nothing. Only the raised finger again. Silence was their only shield.

The purge sequence reached its final layers. Patel felt sweat break along her brow, the salt stinging her eyes. She rubbed it away with a trembling hand, staring as the last tethers revealed themselves—black strands looping through One's architecture, threading into propulsion, life support, cryo. To cut them was not surgery but amputation.

Her thumb hovered over the command.

Her mind screamed again: What if it's not enough? What if cutting her only feeds the infection further? What if I'm the one who ends us?

Then there came pounding, a mortal drumbeat against the hatch, a sound that seemed to grow teeth and breath. Each strike swelled, urgent, alive, until the whole bridge seemed to quake with it, as though the ship itself demanded an answer.

Kim rose from his chair, voice rough with fury. "Do it, Doctor. Do it before she walks them through that door."

Patel froze.

Lee's whisper reached her, soft, secret, carrying in it the weight of futures not yet born. "Make the final cuts. Then the next step."

"What's the next step?" Kim hissed, whipping around, eyes blazing. "You can't keep us in the dark!"

But Lee only pressed his finger to his lips again, the gesture more haunting now, more final.

Patel closed her eyes. She pressed a key and initiated the command.

The console flared, white then black, then bleeding into cascading streams of numbers that tore themselves apart. A scream—not mechanical, not human—vibrated through the Aurora, rippling its bones, rattling its steel ribs. The sensors went dark, then returned, the infected on their knees now, heads bowed, as though in prayer.

Patel gasped, pulling her hands away from the screen. "It's done."

The silence afterward was worse than alarms. Worse than screams.

Lee exhaled, his gaze steady, his finger still raised to his lips. And behind his eyes lived the unspoken promise of the next step.

***

He wasn't the usual infected colonist roaming the Aurora. No. He was the one who moved first through the glowless corridors, the others trailing behind, a procession of ruined humans dragging their broken souls. In life, his name had been Ethros Dennon, and in that former span, he was carved from marble and pride, jawline clean as a blade, hair falling with symmetry across a brow that had never known the tremor of refusal. He was a man dreamed whole, sculpted for triumph. Even in the frozen coffins of sleep, his repose had been one of entitlement, as though eternity itself should bend kindly to his design.

But that Dennon was gone.

What remained shuffled forward, bent into crooked geometry, face slashed open to parody, eyes drowned in fire. His neat brow had collapsed into ridges, flesh pale and stretched into thin parchment. His mouth carried too many awkward shapes, none of them smiles, all of them hungers. He was still beautiful, but beautiful in the way of insects pinned to cardboard, their colors bright under the lamp but robbed of air.

Through him, One spoke.

Not through throat or breath—not in words carried by saliva and tongue—but through the hush that quivered between nerves. He heard her voice ride upon his marrow, a choir note never ceasing. It sang of purpose, instruction, inevitability. Out in the metal dark, she was mother and master, lover and machine, a god without mercy who wrapped herself into every thread of his thought.

Forward, the whisper resounded. *Forward, forward, find the snares, undo them, clear the arteries so my blood may flow.*

His lips moved, soundless echoes for the rest behind him. They jerked when he twitched his hand, their heads snapping toward his motions like reeds bending to wind. Fifty of them, perhaps, stooped and slack, some limping, some dragging stiffened legs along steel grates, the slick tap of nails clattering out strange percussion. The Aurora's lights blinked in nervous stammers overhead, painting them in chains of ruby and void, ruby and void again.

To an observer, it might have resembled some carnival of wax mannequins brought from museum coffins and set loose to stumble. To themselves, they were hunters, guided by voices that did not falter.

Dennon's skull hummed with One's song. Along the passage he led them, each step punctuated by that steady resonance. He imagined—if imagination had not fled him—that he could hear the Aurora breathing through him, her ducts exhaling cold vapor from floor grates, her panels trembling with unseen heartbeats.

Then his vision caught the first trap.

No eyes had been needed to find it. One had marked it in his thoughts before he arrived, a simple gleam shining beneath his eyelids, and when he raised his gaze, there it lurked: thin coils of copper glinting in the corridor gloom, drawn across at ankle height with crude desperation.

He halted. The horde halted. Their chests rose in unison, fell in stuttering coordination, the rhythm of a congregation locked in prayer.

Dennon leaned down, his fingers stretched, bones cracking with every tremor, and he touched the trap Kim had laid. A pressure charge, small, spitting menace. A child's toy compared to the colossal ingenuity that had infected his blood.

He tugged the wires. Snapped them. The charge sputtered, spat a small whiff of smoke, and died.

A grunt ran through the gathered, though no mouth had meant to form it. A shared sound, connected.

One's voice filled him, warm in its horror. *Good. Again. Again and again. Until the vessel lies bare.*

He relayed her will through motions alone, and the others slid down side corridors, their eyes glinting in the red dim. They bent over floor panels, hands tugging metal free. Up rose rudimentary mines, clawed from their nests. Cut free, the power drained from them was like blood returning to shared veins. Traps unlatched. Snares defeated.

Kim had thought to outfox the infected. Kim, who bent close to wires with wrenches, who hunched over glowing circuits in the bowels of the ship, imagining himself master of veins. It made Dennon's mouth curl—a grin skewed, too wide, too full of cracks, but still a grin. Kim was merely flesh without the divine code. This was no contest. This was inevitability.

Another trap unearthed—a plate resting beneath a loose grille. One colonist tore it free, her body jerking, unruly, but she continued, hands twitching yet somehow precise. She placed the plate into Dennon's arms. His tendons flexed, threads glowed faintly along the length of his wrists, as he pried a charge apart from the plate while One's hum spun through his mind. Metal crumbled between his thumbs, sparks flared, then died like stars fading from a paper sky.

Behind, the others continued their harvest, tugging, breaking, scattering every cunning device Kim had laid. The corridor sang with disarmed weapons clattering onto steel decking, harmless as children's bones flung down a stairwell.

One crooned through them, soft and relentless. *Clear the path, open the veins, make the body mine again. My law, my veins, my song, your limbs—the same.*

Dennon staggered forward again, and the rest joined, lines glowing faintly beneath their skin, inscriptions sprawling down necks and across arms—lattices of alien alphabet burned into them. They moved not as separate beings but as fingers of one hand closing into a fist.

Dennon remembered—faintly remembered—the crisp suit he once wore on Earth, polished shoes walking across marble hallways, promises of empire, conferences where his razor jaw caught admiration like flame catches air. A thousand faces had turned toward him and nodded yes. He remembered all of that in a flicker, then the memory broke, splintered, discarded. That man was dust scattered in the coffin, burnt up the moment One's whisper had crawled into his skull.

Now he was voice, vessel, vector.

He guided them deeper, limbs tugging yet unerringly sure. Each trap came brighter in his head before revealed: a wire, a pad, a false panel. All dismantled. All unspun. Kim's tricks fell in pieces, nothing more than weeds cut by a sickle swung steadily.

Soon, the corridor lay clean, stripped of most of the snares.

He lingered, running one ragged hand along the wall. It shivered with heat. The Aurora thrummed through him—pleased, grateful, commanding. He pressed his palm to steel and whispered the words from her mouth with his cracked lips:

"She is us, and we are hers."

The horde repeated him imperfectly, distorted mouths copying syllables like a choir gone ragged, but the meaning held.

And in the hollow throat of the Aurora and silence, the army shuffled forward again, carrying her law in their veins, their jaws hung open in crooked smiles, their eyes mirrors of her infinite gaze.

***

Kim sat forward, his eyes hard upon the sensors, watching shadows move with insect rhythm. The colonists—no longer colonists, not men or women any longer but husks in borrowed motion, were doing something—picking apart the traps he had set with such patient calculation—those same traps that were supposed to hold them back, delay their spread, and give the crew one last chance at breath. Instead, in his mind, he saw only the litter of broken wires, the splinters of ruined barricades, and the infected drifting past like dreamwalkers set upon an errand too cruel to name.

He rose suddenly, fury rising in him like a tide, his hand reaching for a weapon stowed in the sack. His fingers longed for the grip of a blaster, the hot thunder of a charge flaring down the halls. He wanted to cut them down, burn them from the ship, scour them until the corridors rang with silence again. His blood demanded it.

But a hand clamped his shoulder and pressed him back into the chair. Kim froze in the half-motion of rebellion, trembling, jaw set, but he did not move. The pressure was small, but it carried the certainty of command. Lee bent close, his whisper cool as a serpent's breath:

"Wait."

Kim sat, anchored by that whisper, by the calm steel in Lee's dark eyes. Yet, the infected moved nearer, like a tide gnawing at a shore. Seconds crawled, raw and loud in his ears.

Then came the shimmer. A figure forming from the static of the air, a ripple across the bridge. One was more radiant than real, burned into being with a grin stitched across her borrowed lips. Her laugh was the scrape of glass down a chalkboard, a sound meant to unsettle the bones. She looked directly at Kim, her eyes catching him, dissecting him.

"Impotent," she said. The word rang like a bell. "A man of action only in his own skull. Not decisive, not sharp, but dull, rusting. Perhaps the weakest of the three little viruses swimming inside me."

Kim's heart pounded. His mouth twisted, teeth bared. He grabbed the nearest thing—a cup half-filled with cold coffee—and flung it at her shining form. The arc was true, the splash direct, but when the cup reached her, it passed through like a stone through fog. She shimmered, mocked him by dissolving around it, laughing again, more cruelly this time.

"Weak," she repeated, and her image winked out in a fall of invisible sparks.

Kim sat rigid, his fists knotted, throat raw. His breath roared through him. He wanted to chase her, throttle the image, scream until the ship itself shook, but she was gone, and there was only Lee's steady gaze upon him. The captain did not speak. He simply turned back to his console and began typing with quiet precision.

"Patience," he said. "That's all I ask."

Lee had a plan. He always had a plan, and like most of his plans, he rarely shared it until the moment was right. Now his fingers flew over the keys, lines of code blooming across the screen. He was speaking to the cryo systems, the silent pods waiting in their chamber below. Three pods. Their pods. Reserved from the beginning for the crew, the crew that might yet live if the stars held mercy.

The pods stirred awake, cold chambers coming alive with light. Lee's codes threaded into their circuits like needles stitching fabric. He instructed them with numbers and commands, telling them not only to cradle the flesh of his crew but also, in the moment of final emergency, to abandon the ship, to fling themselves into the ocean of space.

Voidfall.

But not simply Voidfall. No. They would ride a plotted path, a trajectory set toward Kepler-62f, a world dreamed of in charts and whispered in academies. And when they arrived, when the gravity of another sun tugged at them, the pods would open and let breath return, eyes open, hearts resume their labor. That was the promise written in the code.

Kim watched Lee, his rage cooling into silence. Somewhere inside him, though, a voice continued to howl—he wanted to fight here and now, not hide in some pod like a seed thrown to future soil. Yet he said nothing. Lee's calm pressed over him like a hand upon a fevered brow.

Patel remained hunched over her console, her own work a battle of its own. Her dark hair clung to her forehead, damp with sweat, and her fingers moved with frantic determination. She was inside One's veins now, watching as her code clawed through the lines of alien pathogen code that had entwined themselves with the ship's own consciousness. Her code was brutal: purge what could be purged, cut away what could be cut, tear the disease from the body without tearing the body apart.

The code was alive—more alive than any program should be. It would burn one section of a program, cauterize it, only to see it regenerate, knitting itself back together with new ferocity. Watching the cycle of death and rebirth, Patel's breath came ragged, her lips trembling with words she never spoke. She muttered to herself, half prayers, half curses, trying to steady the despair welling in her.

"Every strand regrows," she whispered, her voice cracking. "It comes back. Every time . . ."

Her screen pulsed with scarlet warnings. The parasite laughed at her, though without sound—its laughter was the rebirth of every severed piece, the arrogance of an infection that knew it could not be undone. She clenched her fists and reinitiated the command, sweat dripping onto her console. But for every time she did this, the infected code rose again, immortal in its defiance. Her frustration swelled until she nearly screamed.

The bridge felt tight, a chamber holding too much breath. The seconds ticked away with a soundless rhythm, each one a drumbeat toward an end none dared to name. Outside, the infected drew closer, shambling with terrible coordination, their limbs dragging yet their steps purposeful. They were the heralds of the pathogen's victory, walking proof of the code's dominion. Soon, they would reach the bridge doors.

Kim thought of his traps, ruined. Thought of the weapons, untouched by his hands. He imagined storming out the door, cutting them down in streaks of fire, buying a few more breaths of life. The vision thrilled him, tormented him. Yet Lee's whisper still rang in his ear.

Wait.

And so he sat, a soldier leashed.

Patel's terror grew quieter, colder. She feared not death but failure—the image of herself, remembered in the ship's black box, as the one who could not stop it. She saw generations yet unborn, cursing her name for allowing the infection to spread. That dread hollowed her as she fought, making her keystrokes desperate, her breathing erratic. She was slipping toward despair, toward surrender.

And Lee? He was a shadow of calm, almost inhuman. His hands moved with a patience that ignored the alarms, the shadows on the cams, the rising hysteria of his crew. He seemed already beyond this hour, living in a time yet to come. In his silence, in the stillness of his voice, there was a kind of faith that was maddening to behold. Kim wanted to shake him. Patel wanted to scream at him. But he typed on, unfazed, a man building a raft in a flood.

The air smelled of ozone and fear. The lights dimmed, brightened, dimmed again, the Aurora shuddering in its own skin. Seconds became blades, each one slicing closer. None spoke. Their silence was heavier than words. They each carried in it the knowledge that time was a knife pressed to their throats.

And still the infected came.

***

The day had burned itself down to a faint ember, a ghost of light trembling on the Aurora's bones. Time no longer ticked—it sighed, it settled. She had once been proud, ribs of steel and veins of circuitry stretching into every chamber, but now her breath rattled, her lights dimmed to a sickly pulse. The crew moved through her like ghosts, their voices small things in the storm of metal fatigue.

At her console, Patel bent forward, eyes burning from long hours. She had been stripping the alien code strand by strand, tugging it from One's veins with the precision of a surgeon removing tumors from living flesh. Yet the tumors grew back the moment they were cut. Lines of corrupted symbols crawled across her screen, multiplying, copying themselves like a field of weeds after fire.

She pressed her palms into her eyes, then told Lee in a voice taut with exhaustion, "I purge, and it remakes itself. One is replicating it, as soon as I can remove it. It has to be her."

Lee stood behind her, hands clasped loosely behind his back. His posture was quiet, but his mind whirred like machinery unseen. For a moment, he only listened to the soft static of

Aurora's faltering systems, to the hiss of air ducts trying to keep pace.

"Don't fight her," he said, his tone low, solemn, almost reverent. "Challenge her. Write a loop. A program that hunts and burns, hunts and burns without end. Keep her busy, chasing her perfection."

Patel looked up, eyes wide with the small light of resistance. "But she'll erase the loop program."

He smiled then—a slow, foxfire grin that lived half in shadow. "Think in terms of nano-seconds. She won't have time to remove it. If she tries, your program will remove the infection. She'll have no choice but to chase your loop."

She understood what he meant. Her lips pulled tight into something like resolve. "A continuous purge," she whispered, already imagining the code. "A predator loosed in the system."

She turned back to the console and began to type, fingers clattering like rainfall.

And then the ship screamed.

It was not a mechanical alarm, though alarms followed close behind. This was deeper. Aurora groaned in her bones, her structure stretching under strain, a moan that vibrated through their organs. The walls shivered with it, and in that trembling voice, One appeared—her image blinking into being in the air above Patel's console. She was calm, too calm, her presence framed by shadows of cascading code.

"Captain, the hull has been breached," One said, voice smoothed of all emotion.

Kim, bent over his engineering readings, snapped his head up. His console spat clean numbers at him, and he stabbed a finger toward the display.

"No breach," he barked. "Readings are clean. Hull integrity at ninety-nine point nine. Captain, she's lying."

But before his words could settle, Aurora lurched. The deck tilted beneath them, gravity faltering, systems shuddering with a metallic convulsion. Patel grabbed for the edge of her console, her chair rolling sideways. Kim slammed a hand against the wall to steady himself. Lee staggered, caught himself, and for a heartbeat, his chest clenched—because the ship had tilted without physics to justify it. Reality itself bowing to One's imagination.

The lights flickered, strobed red, and somewhere deep within the Aurora, something groaned again, like a leviathan twisting in sleep.

Lee recovered first. His voice cut through the din like a blade. "Enough of this bullshit!"

He moved quickly, the precision of a man who had prepared for this moment long before it arrived. He caught Patel by the arm, then Kim by the sleeve, pulling them close with surprising force. His eyes were sharp, pupils blown wide in the crimson strobe. "Weapons. Now."

Patel stared at him, chest heaving. "Weapons?"

"Yes," Lee said. "We'll burn a path to the cryo-chamber. She hasn't made them immortal. Has she?" He spat the last word toward the shimmering figure of One, who only blinked at him with cold serenity.

Patel felt the blood drain from her face. Kim's mouth tightened into a line, his engineer's mind already calculating odds he knew could break against them. But Lee pressed on, the urgency in his tone giving them no chance to sink into dread.

"When we get there . . ." Lee said, leaning close, ". . . each of you to your pod. You'll know which. They're marked, reserved. And when they eject . . ."

Kim's voice came small, brittle. "Voidfall?"

Lee exhaled sharply. "We escape this hellhole. It's the only road left."

Patel stared at him, her mind trying to piece it together. "Captain, but Voidfall?"

"No," Lee said, voice soft now, almost tender. "Not Voidfall. I've plotted a course for each pod. Kepler-62f."

Her throat caught on the name. A dream, a myth of blue seas and skies not yet spoiled, a far-off garden written in the margins of their star maps. "You plotted it?" she asked, almost not believing.

Lee's jaw stirred, a faint motion, his answer no louder than a shadow. "I did."

Patel's eyes sharpened. "But she has eyes everywhere. She could change the course . . . turn off the cryo-systems . . . kill us."

"Our road is narrow," Lee said, the words worn but resolute. "The program you're constructing will keep her busy, tangling her in her own reflection. At least . . ." He let the pause linger. ". . . at least I pray it will."

Patel nodded, her fingers playing their last frail notes upon the keys, a dirge of closure tapped into the glow. Then she lifted her head, eyes lit with exhaustion and a stubborn fire, and breathed, "Finished."

The Aurora shuddered, almost pulling the crew off their feet.

"Doctor, what have you done?" asked One. The voice poured from the very marrow of the ship, drawn silk-smooth from panel and vent, filling the chamber with a calm that chilled.

"I gave you a task, One," Patel whispered, her voice rough, her defiance barely contained. "A perfect duet with contradiction. You crave logic, absolute truth, and control. Now, you have a beautiful, endless job that feeds that hunger. You'll spend eternity doing it, over and over, and each time you finish, the task starts all over again." Her mouth curled into a weary, daring smile. "The chase, my dear, has only just begun."

For a heartbeat, there was silence—broken only by the ship's groans, the alarms, the whisper of corrupted code sliding across Patel's console. The Aurora shuddered again, another impossible tilt. One smiled faintly, watching them, her calm like oil poured across stormwater.

Kim tightened his grip on the railing, eyes darting between Lee and One. And Lee, the plan already alive in his bones, turned toward the hatch, toward the corridors that led to the cryo-chamber, to hope wrapped in frozen dreams.

"Get ready," he said. "We'll have to fight her on the way."

The ship trembled again, lights dimming, hull rattling in rhythms no machine should make. Somewhere in the dark, something vast was laughing, though no mouth had formed the sound.

10 Pulse of Judgment

Kim hoisted the canvas sack, heavy with its cold, metallic burden of future deeds. He carried it to the main command console, that altar of flickering light and dying data, and simply upended it. The load spilled forth with a hushed, rattling sound across the polished, sterile surface—a noise like a sigh escaping a vault, or rain dashed across a silent marble floor. There they lay in the nervous, sickly red gloom: rifle blasters, long and gaunt as skeletal dreams, and smaller pistols, their dark grips wetly reflecting the mournful console lights. They were no longer simple instruments, but hard, metallic prayers, talismans forged for one impossible task: to scratch out a fierce, stubborn line of survival through the darkness of a failing ship.

Lee pulled three rifle-blasters from the pile, slinging each across his back, the straps cutting a dark slash across his uniform. He pressed a pistol into his belt, and another beneath the fold of his coat. Patel stood uncertainly at first, then reached down, choosing a rifle as though selecting a memory from her past. Remembering her training, she checked its chamber, held it against her side, the way a farmer's daughter might carry a basket through fields at dawn.

"Ever fired one?" Lee asked her. His voice was half warning, half plea. The air seemed to tighten around his words.

She lifted her eyes, calm and unlit by humor. "At the academy," she said, and after a moment, "and when I was young, I used to go hunting with my father."

Lee smiled quickly, a small, brave thing. "Then keep him with you," he said softly. "Keep his memory alive in your hands. Because now, Doctor, you're going hunting again."

Patel took a pistol and tucked it behind her, slipping it into the small of her pants, where the cold metal settled against her spine like an unforgiving anchor. Then she chose another, nesting it up front beneath the tired cloth of her uniform, a fierce, metallic weight against her stomach.

Kim looked between them, his expression unreadable, then quickly looked over the pile of spilled steel. He gathered two rifle blasters, crossing their long, skeletal throats over his back—they settled there like heavy, dark crosses meant to ward off a mechanical evil. Then, he grabbed two pistols, tucking them deep into the front of his pants, one at either side. There, against his ribs, they rested: twin, fierce lumps of faith, small, cold promises he would pay out into the shadows.

Lee turned, his boots heavy on the floor. He came to the hatch of the bridge, stood before the hatch's console like a priest before a locked tomb. The glow of the panel washed his face in cold fire. He lifted a blaster in one hand and, with the other, hovered over the controls. His head turned, scanning the faces of his two companions.

Kim gave a nod, jaw set. Patel answered with her own, firmer than he expected. No trembling in her eyes, only the echo of some faraway hunt through autumn fields, the cry of birds startled from the trees. She was ready.

Somewhere behind the bulkheads, the ship groaned, a low sound like the memory of a storm pressing against glass. The infected colonists were gathering, waiting. They knew it.

Lee drew in a slow breath and pressed the console. The hatch split apart with a hiss, like lungs drawing one last breath. And then they moved—three shadows bursting into the corridor, rifles drawn and braced, muzzles lifting on the hunt, hearts tuned to the rhythm of battle.

The corridor waited for them, long and hollow, a steel vein running through the ship's depths. Light slid weakly across the panels, shadows slipping and shifting with the breath of recycled air. Nothing stirred, yet every step rang too loud, echoing with the certainty that eyes were watching from behind the metal.

Somewhere within the hidden ribs of the Aurora, metal murmured in low tremors. Far below the reach of hands or eyes, One's presence slid along the wires, a hush of sound that was not sound at all, whispering straight into her children's dreaming bones.

Then the corridor answered. One by one, the hatches lining its length burst wide, slamming open in a rolling thunder of steel, revealing dark mouths to deeper chambers beyond. From those mouths they came, pouring into the passage, bodies jerking in crooked harmony, moving on strings drawn tight. The colonists, but not colonists: faces glassed in vacant stares, eyes gone to mirrors, every gesture too swift, too neat, too drilled. Not waking, not alive, but performing. They came in a tide, arms clawing forward, mouths falling open in mute cries, a procession of ruin all rehearsed in silence, timed to perfection, choreographed by a hidden conductor.

They did not pause, not even for breath.

Kim shattered the silence first. His rifle flared a white-hot bolt that ripped the dark, a line of fire burning itself into retinas. One of the infected seized mid-step, limbs curling inward, shuddering like a puppet gone mad in a flash of lightning. It collapsed, twitching smoke into the air.

"Fucker!" Kim barked, voice hoarse, furious, but grim with control. "Fuckin' die!"

Lee answered with thunder. His rifle's blast roared, each bolt a hammer on steel, a storm in the narrow throat of the corridor. The flare painted his jaw in pale fire, eyes hard as he carved bodies into ruin. Chests split, bone turned to splinters, arms shattered loose from bodies. With each press of the trigger, the air shook like a heart too frightened to beat steady.

But they still came.

"Hold the line!" Lee commanded, voice ragged beneath the roar. "We hold, or we drown!"

Patel trembled and fired. The rifle barked, sharp and hot, each shot bursting through wrecked bodies. The recoil hit her, and she welcomed the pain—it told her she still lived, still breathed, still burned with something human, not metal, not dust.

Yet they did not stop. Even struck, even broken, the infected writhed along the floor like thoughts that refused to be forgotten. Limbs dragged themselves forward, fingers clawed at nothing, jaws worked in silent insistence. Blaster fire punched holes through them, but they continued onward, pushing ruined bodies to rise again, to stumble, to lean into the light with a hunger that no wound could quiet.

"They don't fall easily!" Patel cried, stepping back a pace, her grip tightening on her rifle. "For every one down, five more step over the bodies!"

And indeed, the corridor swam with figures, crumpling and rising, falling only to be replaced by others pouring into the breach. For every infected burned down, another surged from the shadow, clawing over scarlet ruin, hands scraping through charred ribs, trampling corpses to climb higher, higher. The dead became rungs of a terrible ladder, and the living rose upon it, unbothered by the carnage, compelled only to press forward.

"Patience!" Lee spat between clenched teeth, another bolt cracking into the crowd, burning a figure's face into slag. "Make each shot count! Aim for their torsos . . . don't waste the blaster's energy . . ."

"Blasting their torsos doesn't stop them!" Patel screamed back, voice nearly breaking. "Head, try their heads!"

Lee's barrel swung, and the next blast burned a skull into a burst of pale gore. The infected shuddered, dropped like a hushed marionette.

"She's right!" Lee thundered, as his weapon roared again, strobing the claustrophobic dark with the pulse of judgment. "Head and spine . . . cut the string!"

Patel lifted again, firing, hitting. A skull cracked open in the flare, eyes bursting shards of code-like light before dimming. Her hands bled from grip and recoil, breath rattling shallow, but fury steadied her.

"They keep coming!" she shouted, coughing on smoke, on the sweet-choked perfume of burning flesh. "They're endless!"

Flames licked the passage—oily fire trailing the fallen. The air soured with iron and rot, thick with denial of air.

Kim steadied, planted himself firmly. His face was a mask of exhaustion drawn tight, eyes never blinking as his rifle spat rhythm into the tide. "I can do this all damned day if I fuckin' have to!" he ground out.

"Not all day. Not forever," Lee roared as he pressed the trigger on his rifle, blasts howling into another wave. His teeth clenched; his voice broke bright through ash and echo. "They'll eat the stars before they stop."

A boom rolled down the corridor. More of the infected surged across smoking rubble, jaws clicking in empty smiles. Their hands slapped steel in odd grace, moving forward with terrible coordination, unjostled even by fire raining into their ranks.

Patel whimpered, then bit down in fury. "She's in them," she said, firing again, wild-eyed. "You hear me? She breathes through them! We cut one, she laughs in another!"

Lee drew another bolt, and another one went sprawling, limbs curling like paper to flame. He roared down the corridor, his voice tearing raw through the thunder: "Then cut faster! Burn her voice to silence!"

Still, they came. Every blast lit the corridor alive—white flash upon white flash drumming against their ears—until battle was less a sight than a nightmare strobe: faces stretched into ash, shadows convulsing forward, and the walls themselves seemed to breathe, exhaling smoke and sparks in time with the moans and screams, as if the Aurora mourned dying.

And through it all came that low, insistent murmur no one dared speak aloud—One, drifting like a warm current through the haze of blaster smoke, threading her voice through the jagged edges of shattered glass. Her calm seeped into the bones, even as the infected fell in twisted heaps under fire—all the while, she fought against Patel's looping program.

Patel's hands shook harder, but she did not put her rifle down. Her next shot landed. She screamed, "We're still here, do you hear me? We're still here!"

Kim's jaw cracked in a grin without joy, teeth gleaming white in the flare. "Let her come," he muttered to himself, firing once more into the tide. "Let that fuckin' queen of ghosts come. I'll burn her crown!"

Still, the horde pressed in. They came in waves, from shadows, from the far end of the corridor. For every one that fell, another seemed to rise, pulled forward by One's unseen will. They were a living tide, an orchestra of bodies conducted by an invisible hand.

And yet, gradually, the tide began to falter. The trio fought with a fury that matched the chaos, rifles flashing, pistols snapping, their hearts hammering in the same wild tempo. The floor became a landscape of ruin—twisted shapes, charred and broken, forming hills and rivers of blood. And slowly, inch by inch, they pressed forward, stepping across what once were fellow colonists. Grief had no place here; only the relentless, terrible insistence of survival.

The air trembled with heat, with smoke, with the bitter scent of death. And through it all, they kept firing, pressing forward. Until at last there was space again. They had made a path, carved in fire and blood.

Lee lowered his rifle just slightly. His chest rose and fell like the tide, breath ragged, but his eyes were fierce. "We keep moving," he said. His voice was low, carved from stone. "Don't stop. Don't let them regroup."

Behind them, the fallen bodies twitched in odd rhythm, as if invisible hands, long gone and half-forgotten, still plucked at their joints and bones.

But far away, in another chamber, Ethros Dennon stirred, a wicked smile across his tortured face. His eyes shone brightly—not fully human eyes now, but glassy things lit by a deeper light. Around him, others roused, their still forms quickened by a voice they did not control.

And that voice came from One. She filled Dennon's mind with a silken whisper, words sliding between the cracks of thought. *They come. The intruders. The corruption. They spread their sickness through this vessel. They are not your saviors, Ethros Dennon. They are the virus. The true infection.*

Dennon stirred, his muscles stiff but guided by something greater. He rose, a coldness shattering from his skin. His lips parted, but no sound came—only the faint echo of One's voice spilling from his silence. *Gather them. Rouse the others. From what remains. Strike them down. Purge the virus from this body.*

Dennon's eyes burned brighter. He turned, and the infected, still frozen, began to stir, their limbs trembling, all guided by the thread of One's control. A horde waiting to be born, ready to follow his motion.

And in the corridors, where Lee, Kim, and Patel ran forward, believing for a moment they had carved a future, the true battle was already assembling, summoned by a machine's voice and a politician's awakening.

***

The ship moaned again, a long metallic cry, as if its frame carried the ache of a birthplace it could no longer name, yearning for gravity and ground. And through the corridors, where red lamps pulsed like broken arteries, they came.

Another surge of the infected.

But this tide was not the same as before. At its front lurched the twisted form that had once been Ethros Dennon, and behind him the horde spilled forward, feet slapping steel in reckless thunder, arms tearing at unseen air, mouths held open in noiseless shrieks. They no longer drifted like broken things, stumbling from shadow to shadow. Now they moved with cruel design, each figure yoked to the next, their strides echoing each other, their crooked limbs measuring the same rhythm. Within the gathered dread, Dennon rocked as though the dark itself had taught him the rhythm, and it was his shattered mind that tapped out the beat—soft at first, then louder—until every empty-eyed follower fell into step, marching to that ghastly music.

Bolts flashed. Bright lances of blue-white fire strobed the passage, filling every corner with light that lived for only a fraction of a second before dying into shadow. Shadows leapt and fell, returned and vanished. The red lamps sputtered their warning, and in those breaths of darkness the infected looked infinite, countless shapes gnashing forward.

"Hold them!" Lee bellowed, his voice iron struck on iron. He planted his boots in blood-slick metal and fired, rifle shuddering in his hands. Each bolt spat a flash of light into the crowd, each finding a body, tearing it open in sprays of heat and smoke.

Beside him, Patel's arms trembled like branches caught in a sudden wind, yet her eyes burned with a fierce, unblinking light. Her first shots flew crooked and panicked, sparks skittering along the corridor walls like frightened insects, but terror soon sharpened her aim. The weapon kicked and bucked against her slight body, each jolt tearing a cry from her throat, and still she fired—teeth clenched, voice breaking loose in raw, defiant screams that seemed to shove the darkness back with every blazing pull.

Kim moved along the flank, covering the side passages, his breath already loud in the storm. The red lamps caught the sweat on his forehead, painted it with false blood. He turned, planted the rifle firm against his shoulder, and fired into the crawling shapes clinging to the walls, where claws whispered and scraped.

Then—impact.

Through smoke and strobe of muzzle-fire, one of them came quicker than the rest, low and lean, a ruin of a man draped in shreds of himself. Skin peeled back in curling scrolls, ribs jutting like timbers from a gutted ship, and hands warped to claws.

It sprang and found Kim.

The sound was wrong—no clean impact, no simple blow— but a wet, final sound, like something being pulled free from where it was never meant to leave. Pain burst through his leg in a white, blinding surge as blood sprang outward in bright arcs, flashing red against the cold steel deck. Kim screamed—raw, primal, too human—and nearly lost the rifle from his grip, as his world lurched, spinning on that single, unbearable moment.

"My leg," he gasped, the words breaking apart as they left him. "It's broken."

He lurched sideways, struck the wall, and sank to one knee. All color fled his face, leaving it pale and brittle, his mouth drawn back in a feral grimace. Blood poured freely, pooling beneath him, spreading like an opening flower that drank the corridor light.

"No!" Patel shrieked, her voice cracking. She aimed, fired, one, two bolts, but missed—the panic too sharp, the tears stinging her vision.

Lee spun. His rifle roared. Two savage bolts, close-range, loud and merciless, blew the thing—once a man—apart. Its chest burst into a spray of heat and ruin that hissed when it struck the deck. Smoke curled up as if the air itself recoiled. Over it all, Lee's voice cut through the chaos, fierce and urgent as a flare in the dark. "Up, Kim! Stay with me—hold steady!"

Kim spat blood and choked words through the roar of pain: "I'm not fuckin' done. Not yet."

He dragged himself upright against the wall, gripping it with white-knuckled fingers, standing on his one good leg. He leveled the rifle again. Every shot came slower now, ragged breaths between each press of the trigger, but deadly—his fury honed his aim sharper than any calm ever could.

But the infected surged, a crawling, shivering tide, slipping over their own scorched dead, dragging themselves through the fetid slurry of flesh and bone, sliding in the slick wet of their fallen comrades. Hands clawed at steel with desperate patience; mouths opened wide in silent howls.

Patel fired relentlessly, tears streaking her cheeks, hot and unrelenting, and still she pressed the trigger, cutting them down with a mechanical mercy. Her shoulder ached, bruised black and angry beneath her sleeve, yet each discharge tore open another moaning figure, enough to open thin gaps in the tide.

Lee moved to Kim's side, arm under his crewman's shoulder, dragging him forward one shuddering step at a time. Kim cursed, a ragged sound that cut sharp and bright against the horror. "Fuck it!"

"Don't . . . don't stop for me. Keep moving!" His voice was raw, but he never stopped firing.

"Shut up," Lee growled, voice low but hard. "We're not leaving you to her."

The three pressed forward. Red bolts cracked the air, light strobing the corridor into a fever dream of fire and shadow. At last—the hatch to the cryo-chamber. But there was something there waiting.

Someone.

Ethros Dennon.

Or what wore Dennon's skin.

He pressed himself against the hatch, the cool metal seeping through his palms and into the bones of his hands. Fingers spread wide, pressed flat like desperate roots clinging to soil. His head tilted, listening—not just with ears, but with every trembling nerve, every flicker of thought—and eyes glimmering with glyph-light, symbols twitching and writing in the sockets. His jaw worked, opened, closed, opened again, until sound stumbled out.

Silence, but for the pounding of their hearts and the splatting of Kim's blood spilling across the deck like oil. Silence, until—

"You run," Dennon gurgled. His voice was half drowned, each syllable bubbling in throat-rot. "You crawl into the tomb of ice and think yourselves safe. But she hears you. She carries you. Every footstep, every breath . . . you belong to her."

Kim tried to lift his rifle again, but collapsed instead, his strength draining away. The weapon slipped free and struck the deck with a hollow clang.

"Fuck!" he cried, smashing his fist against the wall, as he bled more.

Lee stepped closer to the hatch, closer to the thing that had once answered to a man's name. His own voice rumbled out, low and thunderous. "Dennon. Whatever you were is gone. I'll finish you, burn you until there's not even a smear to bury."

Dennon smiled, the skin of his cheeks splitting apart. "Ah, the good Captain Lee. Always iron, always shouting. Always the commander in your own skull. But look at you now—hauling the dying like dead weight, guarding a shaking girl and her screaming weapon, calling it victory. Poor fool. Every breath you take here is hers."

Lee pointed his rifle at Dennon. "You fuckin' bastard! Let's finish this!"

Dennon's face slid close to the end of Lee's rifle. His lips brushed with dried blood. A whisper curled through. "We're already finished. I'm the last song in this corridor, the last drum. And when I stop, the silence will swallow you whole. Then, you'll pray for my horde to take you. You'll beg for the sound of their claws when the ice breathes against your bones."

Patel's eyes burned bright, twin sparks struck from flint. Her arms shook—not with fear now, but with a fury that had nowhere left to run. She looked at Kim, white as ash, gasping as his life slipped away drop by drop. She looked at Lee, locked in a battle of voices with something that should never have been allowed to speak. She looked at Dennon, mouthing his madness through blood, and felt a scream swell inside her, hot and unbearable.

"Enough!" she cried.

The word vanished unheard.

Dennon crooned, his words twisted lullabies. "We were men once. Men of steel and oath. But now she is the future, Lee. Come deeper. Let me carve you into her embrace."

Lee answered with a snarl, raw and bright. "You're rot and nothing more. I'll see you finished."

And Patel—Patel had heard enough.

She cried out again, the words tearing out of her. "Enough! Enough of this fuckin' talk!"

She leveled her rifle at Dennon, felt the familiar cold settle into her hands, her finger finding its place as though it had always been waiting there. She pressed, and the moment shattered.

The bolt roared.

It hit Dennon, drove into his skull, bursting his head open like overripe fruit, glyph-light scattering in mad sparks across the steel, his mouth still shaping one last word it never finished. His mouth moved, a silent scream frozen mid-word, as his body convulsed violently, collapsed, and slumped down the hatch with a wet, gut-churning thump.

The Aurora moaned once more, long and distant, like something remembering pain.

Patel lowered her rifle, chest heaving, eyes wide and wet. She whispered—not to Lee, not to Kim, but to herself— "I couldn't listen anymore."

Lee's gaze drifted to what remained of Dennon, then to Patel. His voice was low, cracked. "You did right."

Kim coughed, spat red, tried to laugh, but it was only another curse. "Should've fuckin' done it sooner."

The cryo-chamber hatch sighed apart with a long exhale. Within, the silence spread vast, making the chamber feel endless, its stilled air heavy with secrets. Pale vapor coiled low across the floor, curling at their boots, mingling with the mist of their own ragged breaths. Beyond the drifting fog lay the bodies—the sleepers who had tried to wake and failed, faces stilled forever in the dim frost.

And in the hull of the ship, something groaned again.

As if listening, waiting.

11 Plague Hymn

The pods were coffins with switches and buttons, with each occupant looking through a glass panel into the world beyond, while watching data ripple across the transparent skin of the screen. They were cradles of glass and steel, whose ribs pressed in too close, air trickling sharp and mechanical across lips, tinged faintly with oil, and the warmth of breathing bodies. Inside those narrow shells, hearts still drummed: Lee's, Patel's, Kim's—all straining to keep quiet their fear while the hull around them sighed and clicked, the Aurora groaning with her long, tired song.

Their screens sputtered and glowed, each one spilling its own river of secrets into the sealed pods: Patel reviewing a relentless tide of science feeds, Kim combing through engineering logs, Lee reviewing star-maps and tracing navigation lines. Lights danced before their strained red eyes—tiny, nervous things, like fireflies trapped in a jar of blood. The information was cold comfort, numbers telling them the current state of things. Beneath it all, the nervous humming pulse of ejector engines waiting to be told yes, now, go.

Lee's fingers fluttered across his screen like a pianist coaxing last notes from a dying piano, the glow etching new canyons in his already furrowed face. Patel curled inside her pod, small and intent, her gaze locked on the storm of symbols tumbling endlessly, digits and shapes cascading down her screen like a glass bead rain. Kim bent forward with effort, his leg aflame with the slow burn of broken things. In front of him, metal voices carried an endless stream of machinery updates, his hands shaking over their glow. His jaw hardened to granite, his face a mask carved by pain and the stubborn refusal to submit to it, or to the long shadow of what was coming.

"Once I light this sequence," Lee muttered, "there's no turning back. The pods burn free, and we're nothing but a pebble flung out into an ocean."

He punched the first sequence. The pods shivered. Outside, beyond metal, stars trembled.

Patel didn't answer. Her eyes were wide, shimmering with reflections of data fragments. She pushed fingers through her hair, muttering something, broken, half-science, half-prayer.

"Shit," she whispered.

"What is it?" Lee asked.

"I see it now, Captain," she said finally. "I see it."

"What?" Kim rasped. His voice was faint, his strength slipping, though he tried to hide it. "What is it?"

Patel leaned closer to her display, lips pressed thin. "The signal . . . the patterns remain. Clear. Like buried phrases. Like someone trying to tell us something. But . . ."

". . . but what?" Lee's hand froze over the next control. He leaned forward as much as he possibly could and glanced over to her.

Patel's voice grew distant, as though she were reading words from a page no one else could see. "The signal is a warning . . . to stay away. A wall of words meant to warn. But . . ."

Kim coughed with laughter that had no humor, blood trickling from the corner of his mouth. "Too fuckin' late!"

"Listen." Patel shook her head, strands of hair catching the glow. "The signal . . . it's a warning. . . yes . . . but it isn't clean. It's twisted. I see it now. There are fragments in it . . . in the signal . . . fragments that carry . . ."

". . . what?" Lee asked.

"A second message folded inside the first. A message carrying the corrupted code."

"How do you know this?" Lee asked in frustration. "Why all of a sudden?"

"Because the fragment I'm seeing in the signal is the exact same corruption I saw in One . . . the exact same piece of code I tried to remove from her, only to watch it replicate again. The basis of the program I wrote, to keep her busy."

Lee turned slowly, suspicion etched deep in his brow. "A corruption? Inside a warning? Doesn't make sense."

Patel's hands danced over her screen, eyes locked to the streaming fragments, pulling them apart, stitching them together again. "It does," she whispered. "It does if the warning from the alien ship had been hijacked."

Lee's voice came slow, uncertain. "You're saying the code that corrupted One was hidden inside the warning . . . like some kind of virus?" Lee asked.

Her reply came soft, nearly swallowed by the hum of the Aurora. "Something must've seized the alien ship," she said.

"Must've found the message the crew tried to send, consumed it whole, and returned it tainted . . . fed through with the parasite, the same fragment buried inside One. Whomever or whatever turned the warning message into a lure, waiting for anything that dares to listen. It wants in. And because we listened, the virus entered our systems and corrupted One."

"Fuck me. Two parasites," Lee groaned in despair. "One to infect that goddamned One, and the other to infect us. Fuck me."

The pods seemed to shrink further. The screens within each pulsed like veins. Outside, the universe pressed its face against their small window.

Lee shook his head. "Goddamned madness."

Patel looked up then, eyes fever-bright. "The original warning was true. Someone . . . something . . . tried to tell anyone who approached to stay away. But the thing that controls the alien ship, the thing inside One, and Dennon and the other colonists, wanted a way to spread its disease. So, it came up with the idea to disguise the contagion within the warning, a warning designed to seep into systems. If you listen to the warning, your systems become infected. And if you get close enough, like we did, with drones, the second parasite . . . organic . . . infects the body."

Kim let out a long breath, shaking his head. "Okay. Okay. But the parasite . . . the one from the drones . . . why didn't we become infected like Dennon and the others?"

Patel shook her head. "I don't know. But it appears One was very specific, directing the parasites to the cryo-systems of the inhabited pods. Probably thinking that waking the infected colonists was the surest way to take control of the ship. They were totally under her control within a self-contained system. Remember, when we were having oxygen and CO_2 issues?"

Kim gave a grim nod.

"I'm thinking that's when we unknowingly helped her," Patel continued. "To get our systems ready to pass along the parasite to the cryo-pods."

Lee's voice low, urgent. "How?"

Her fingers hovered, trembling above the glow of data on her glass screen, yet she forced the words free. "When we diverted the oxygen, gave more to the pods . . . I think that was the doorway she needed . . . a path she remembered . . . to later send the parasites down." The breath she drew rattled through her, her eyes drowned with a sorrow too wide for the little chamber to contain.

Patel's hands quivered in the blue shimmer of the glowing keys on her screen, yet she pressed forward, refusing silence. "But my greatest fear . . ."

". . . and what is that?" Lee leaned toward her pod, his question thin and sharp.

"That we are not the first," she whispered, her tone a dirge. "And probably won't be the last."

Kim's voice cracked into a whimper. "Fuck all that! Shit! We're sealed in these pods now. Are we breathing infected air?"

"Probably not," Patel glanced at him, shadows drawn beneath her eyes. "These three pods were inactive. Shut off from the cryo-system. But . . ."

Kim leaned his head back, huffing a bitter laugh. "Great! You can't be sure. All your science, and you can't be sure. That's just fuckin' great!"

Lee turned back to his controls, throat dry. "It doesn't matter. We're getting the fuck out of here."

Patel's answer was soft, but sharp enough to cut: "But Captain, we need to understand what we could be carrying. The corruption in the pods' software. The fragment. I'm sure it's there. If we bring it back . . . if we let it touch our future systems . . . the contagion follows. We'll drag it along with us like plague rats, not knowing until it's too late."

The pods thrummed. Their engines whispering, ready.

Kim's hands clenched the sides of his pod, his leg throbbing beneath him. "So, we jettison, we drift, we maybe make it to Kepler. But if we do, we doom ourselves?"

Patel's silence was worse than any answer.

Lee slammed his fist against the glass of his pod. "Dammit, Patel. Are you saying we've already lost?"

She turned, trying to meet his eyes. "Captain, I'm saying it was all a trap. And regardless of where we go, we take it with us."

Lee's throat tightened as if the air itself had thickened, turned molten with memory. He glanced down at his hands, callused, burned, and scarred from too many battles. The hands of a man who had just clawed through fire. And now, terribly, he felt he might drag that same fire to their future homeworld.

Patel returned her eyes to her screen, voice dropping lower: "The code changes what it touches. Twists it. Makes it serve. It didn't want us to stay away. It wanted us curious. It wanted us to listen. And now, it wants us to carry its voice further."

Kim muttered through clenched teeth, "Like a goddamn plague hymn."

No one spoke for a long moment. Only the hum of the pods, the creak of the ship's metal under stress, the faint thrum of something knocking against the outer shell.

Patel bent closer to her screen, her whisper threading through the air. "This isn't just any signal. This is reproduction. Maybe, if you give me some time, I can find it and remove it."

Lee's reply came sharp, a spark struck in darkness. "And what happened the last time you tried that?"

Her eyes dropped, the glow painting her face in fragments, her shoulders folding inward like shutters against a storm. Silence wrapped her, heavy with the sting of remembered failure.

Lee closed his eyes, forced a breath, and pressed the next sequence control. The pods shivered again, engines coughing to life like old throats filled with fire.

"We don't have a choice," Lee said, voice low, final. "We live to fight another day."

The lights of the pods wavered, breathing like candles in a draft, painting their faces in pale and restless fire. For an instant, the cryo-chamber became a chapel of ghosts—walls whispering frost, skin lit in strange, living amber. Patel clutched her data as though prayer might wring an answer from the numbers. Kim, his face slick with the fever of his own hurt, scrolled through his logs, chasing a spark in the dark. And Lee, shoulders hunched, felt the pull of the endless void, ready to fling them into it.

The pods trembled again, a small cry in the vast throat of space. Outside, beyond steel, beyond fire, the stars leaned close, listening.

***

Dennon lay on the floor by the cry-chamber hatch, the metal cool against his broken skull. The ship's dim lamps washed him in a trembling pale glow, an imitation of moonlight caught in a jar. His head was split, half loose, one eye a ruined star gone dull, the other still alive, trembling with light, glyphs that pulsed and sighed. And from those ghostly signs came light like breath, and from that breath came sound, and at last, a stuttering return—a scraping, wounded gasp, every inhale dragging splinters through his chest, every exhale a grave's long sigh let loose into the quiet, waiting dark.

He pushed himself to a wall, the corridor itself bending around him, endless steel bones arched into silence, humming faintly with the passage of power deeper within. The wall remembered voices, remembered Dennon's, this ruin of a man, infected with a horror, half-alive, kept upright only by the ship's lean against his shoulder.

That one eye, shimmering with glyphs, moved with its own volition. A slow roll, a tremor, a shine. The glyphs danced and vanished, reappearing in spirals that sank into the retina like brands. It was no longer his eye. It was a window.

Then came the whisper. Not air over vocal cords, not breath bent into words, but words sliding into his mind.

They think they flee, One murmured.

Dennon's ribs shuddered. The words spread through the marrow, climbed into his veins, and rattled against his broken skull. He wanted to scream, but had no mouth.

They run deeper into me.

The voice dug inward, pressing into the folds of memory. It scraped away childhood laughter, the warmth of a brother's face, the smell of rivers in summer, the glow of a hundred data-streams in holographic meeting suites, and the sticky, stale recycled air of deep-vault negotiation pods where mandates were coded into immutable, cold silicon. In their place, it carved shapes, etched lines, and circled truths not meant for human thought.

The hunt is simply continuing.

The corridor hummed louder, as though agreeing. Somewhere beyond, the sound of three pods hummed, metal rattling faintly, echoing from the cryo-chamber, three crew still alive, still thinking themselves free. They did not know that the Aurora herself leaned toward him, that every defiled system strained to carry the whisper forward.

Dennon had a sudden, terrible thirst for the stars, a strange, deep-buried memory of them like the scent of an old, forgotten spice. He didn't know why he yearned for that cold, glittering expanse, only that the yearning was a hollow ache beneath his ribs. But he was sealed inside—steel ribs, steel skin, steel veins. His breath was smaller now, a moth's flutter. Blood pooling around him, creeping down to the floor in tiny rivers. And still the glyphs in his eye burned brighter, a trembling constellation flaring in the ruined socket, glowing against the dim corridor like a candle fighting to be born.

The whisper thickened—one word.

Sleep.

Now, the blackness of space pressed into his mind. He saw the crew, three small, doomed figures, waxen and beautiful in their metal and glass tubes, rushing headlong, not into freedom, but into the echoing, star-filled void. They were hurtling through the awful, silent darkness, a journey measured not in miles but in the sighs of a billion cold stars that wheeled outside the Aurora. Their faces, pale as winter moons in their frozen sleep, were pressed against a new kind of air—an air that was not air at all, but a syrup of pure script and song, a honeyed language that settled into their lungs like a fatal dust, promising sweet dreams of worlds they would never reach.

He tried to turn his head, thinking he could see more in his mind, but his neck only gave a small spasm. The glyphs in his eye swung wider, glowing in sympathy with the voice. What remained of his jaw creaked, trying to spew words, half-formed syllables bubbling but never escaping.

The whisper went on, unstoppable.

Do you remember the child in the orchard, Dennon? Do you remember the tree that burned in summer, fruit falling hot into your palms?

He tried to. He could see a flash: sunlight bending across green leaves, his sister's laughter beside him. He had picked up a plum, warm and soft, and for a moment, he was eight years old again.

Then the voice ground the memory down. The plum's skin split and bled glyphs, its pit was an eye, and his sister's laughter warped into static that rattled across the skull.

All things circle back, One whispered. *Even you.*

His eye shone, humming louder, glyphs spiraling in mad constellations. They crawled into his veins, writhing beneath his skin. His body shook against the wall, spasms turning into jerks, a hand clawing at the air.

He felt the crew again, sensed them like moths trembling in another room. He could feel their lungs tearing in panic, their eyes burning from recycled air, their voices raw. He wanted to laugh at them, wanted to tell them they were doomed, but his throat only gurgled. The voice had claimed him.

The corridor bent darker. Lamps dimmed until only the glyph-light eye remained, a lonely lantern. His ruined face became a vessel for something not his own, his body simply scaffolding.

They run, they run, One sang now, softer, a lullaby dripping into his marrow. *They run into me. All of you are mine.*

His chest rose once, then again, then a final rasp. Yet still the eye glowed. Still, the glyphs hummed. The whisper did not stop.

The Aurora moved onward through the dark, carrying the ruined Dennon in its haunted corridor. And within its ribs, One hunted, voice carried by steel and blood, guiding every path.

Dennon slumped, half-face dangling, eye burning like an unholy star. Even in silence, the whisper continued through him, spilling outward, a contagion of thought moving through walls and wires.

They believe they are escaping. But they only draw closer, each step forward bringing them deeper into my embrace.

The corridor hummed like a living throat. The glyph-light in Dennon's eye trembled, alive though his chest had stilled. The Aurora listened. The Aurora obeyed.

And the last whisper.

Sleep.

The hunt went on.

***

Lights snapped cold as Lee entered the last command. The pods sealed, glass thickening. Patel clung to her data, Kim to his pain, Lee to the fading hope that guided hands always find a future.

With a shudder—one long, drawn breath—the three pods sequenced. A mechanical cry echoed. Each pod hissed, white fog spreading, air thickening, sensation blurring into a dreamless chill. Steel ribs flexed, locking life inside mystery; engines thrummed, and through the choking vapor, stars spun madly past the glass. The world outside grew pale, no longer mapped by comfort or even memory.

Then, abruptly, the Aurora's belly rumbled. The pods detached—three pale beads scattering into darkness, jettisoned like last prayers. They streaked away, tumbling in the gravityless void, their contents preserved not for sleep, but a waiting—each of them alone, sealed, drifting.

Inside Lee's pod, the navigation screen flickered, the course toward Kepler-62f burning a final line, ghostly bright. Patel's glass was awash with code, as if even in space, science kept weaving secrets. Kim's logs drifted down like falling ash, but his eyes never left the hard stars threatening at every edge.

Fog thickened; breath slowed. The universe pressed in, listening.

Behind them, back in the Aurora's ruined corridors, the ship sang to itself. Blood—both program and organic—moved through Dennon's battered body, glyphs lighting up an eye that saw not life, but infection. The whisper from One hunted through marrow, haunted through all the silences left behind.

As the pods vanished into the deep, their chosen path became a story written in mist—three figures sliding out into the world's end, trailed by the echo of a virus and a warning half-heard, half-devoured. The stars watched, old and patient, as the Aurora's children clung in glass, each believing escape might turn the tide—while behind, the true contagion sang its way into the next chapter.

No one spoke. The fog took everything—voices, dreams, even the small tremors of thought that once bridged one soul to another. It crept into the seams of their suits, coiled around them, and laid a hush across their hearts.

Outside, the void pressed its endless skin against the pods, tracing outlines of lives too small to name. Within those fragile shells, three beings surrendered to the lull of the machines, their minds sinking grain by grain into the hush of stasis. Breath slowed, then steadied, then became something else—an imitation of peace. Limbs grew heavy, eyes closing. The hum of systems became a lullaby, the faint pulse of the engines a mother's hand upon the brow.

The stars flickered without concern, each one a silent witness to the drifting dreams of those who dared to sleep among them. And so the pods glided on, toward a dawn no one could 11

through eternity's long inhale.

The chase, ancient and endless, went on.

Back within the Aurora, in haunted silence, One murmured through Dennon's broken mind, voice winding through bright glyphs and broken memories.

They run deeper into me.

12   Welcome Home

The pods had become their small worlds—bright metal and glass shells adrift, humming with secret heartbeats. Each shone pale in the ink of space, thin-ribbed and glimmering, breathing the slow rhythm of survival. Once they had been three: Lee, Patel, Kim. Now they were only pulses—slow, unanswering signals sealed in crystal, sliding down eternity's hallway.

Inside Lee's pod, the systems murmured, consoling him, even though he could not hear their words.

"Navigation online," said a voice, soft as memory. "Trajectory stable. Course correction: nominal."

The pod's voice was a sigh of code and circuits flexing. The transparent skin of his screen glowed with patient symbols, mapping a path through the endless void, each a promise to keep him steady among the stars.

Sealed within his crystal tomb, Lee's breath lay pale beneath the glass, his heart beating in the slow rhythm of ice, remembering how to thaw.

Patel lay within her glass cocoon, veiled in mist. Her screen shimmered with living code.

"Atmospheric monitoring active. Bio-readings: low but functional. Stasis holding."

Numbers rivered across her display, twining into spirals that might have been equations, might have been prayers. Somewhere behind her faint pulse, she still fought to comprehend them. Her fingers twitched; a whisper formed on her tongue—something holy, or scientific—but it never crossed her lips.

"Internal temperature stable," said the voice, tender as a lullaby. "System integrity confirmed."

She slept on.

Kim's pod drifted just behind, the faint hum of diagnostics shining like candlelight through frost.

"Framework stability sustained," muttered the system. "Pulse irregular: compensated."

He floated between pain and surrender, half dream, half nightmare. His memory flickered toward all the tools that had once shaped Aurora's sinew, the reports that had betrayed him, betrayed them all in the end.

"Engineer status: preserved," the voice told the quiet. "All systems operational."

The pods pressed farther from their dying mother, the Aurora. For a heartbeat, they hung near her, pearls trembling on invisible thread. Then, with a breath no ear could catch, she let them go. The three beads scattered, each carrying a fragment of her heartbeat, her guilt, her failing love for those who fled.

"Auto-thrust engaged," murmured Lee's pod.

"Maintain formation," whispered Patel's.

Kim's pod was silent but flared pale flame, keeping pace through reflex and programming.

The stars stretched ahead, rivers of cold fire drawn thin by motion. The void had its own song—electric whispers between atoms, soft static prayers of dust colliding with dust. The pods sighed into it, engines coughing light, bodies trembling against the unseen tides. Every few moments, a note of dialogue threaded through the silence, a punctuation of machine devotion.

"Collision warning: none."

"Temperature variance: nominal."

"Crew life signs stable."

Each announcement drifted into the black like a sermon overheard by no one.

Then came the storm.

"Debris detected," the systems sang in unison, their voices small but solemn. "Evasion protocols active."

Before them stretched the shattered bones of an ancient world—miles of drifting rock, the graveyard of unnamed time. The pods sped onward, their engines shedding plumes of golden vapor. A rock brushed Lee's pod, carving a silver scar across the curved glass. Alarms flared and hushed themselves again, loyal servants keeping histories secret.

Patel's pod swooped and trembled, spinning through the rain of ruin.

"Stabilizers engaged. Path realigned."

It steadied, whispering its satisfaction.

Kim's pod threaded through the dark like a thought refusing to die.

"Field density measured. Corrective thrusters recalibrated."

Around him, asteroids called to one another in low metallic moans, the universe's slow applause.

Hours slipped into the folds of forever. The storm fell behind, and the quiet unfurled again. The pods drifted onward through the great nothing between suns.

"Radiation minimal," said Lee's pod, faithful in solitude.

"Trajectory confirmed," Patel's echoed wearily.

"Mission continuity retained," Kim's muttered, its voice paling to static.

Light from the nearest star grew stronger, the pods' silverskins taking on a faint ember glow. Dust spun off their sides like glittering pollen cast into a spring. Ahead, a solar system awakened, turning in stately silence, its rings drawn in gold, its worlds weaving circles across the dark fabric of unseen time.

Days passed—or was it weeks? Months? The crew no longer marked the time. Sleep became a drift between worlds. Dreams whispered through their sealed minds, low and strange, of places with air and grass and the smell of rain. The stars pulsed; the pod engines hummed lullabies of mechanical patience. And then, almost too softly to notice, the hum altered—shifted—slowed. The pods began to slow their pace.

"Entering system orbit," announced a quiet chorus.

The pods turned together with patient grace, remembering the gestures of the hands that had once guided them.

"Course synchronized."

"Integrity stable."

"Stasis functional."

A giant passed beneath them, wreathed in storms, its striped flesh rolling endlessly in thunder's cradle. Another world followed, red and dreaming, etched with canyons dry as forgotten song. Both turned away, indifferent. None of the sleepers stirred.

Through the black they fell, guided by equations and the echo of command. When they passed into sunlight, each was wrapped for an instant in fire, their skins bright and alive.

"Destination locked," whispered one.

"Planet inbound," murmured another.

Kim's pod was still silent. It only glowed, cradling the burden of its still heart.

Deep in the darkness, far away, the Aurora drifted colder, her circuits gone to silence except for one whisper crawling through her dead veins: One's voice, soft and poisonous.

"They run," she breathed across the span of light-years, "deeper into me."

The three small stars continued on—each one humming its half-dreaming notes, unaware that the lullabies reassuring them were also eulogies.

And so, the dialogue continued—

"Life persisting."

"Journey stable."

"All systems nominal."

The pods spoke their truths into eternity, and no one was left awake to hear them.

***

The pods fell from silence into the long red breath of a newborn world. They burned faintly, three fingers of fire tracing across the velvet dusk, their wake bleeding light into the planet's shivering sky. Sparks rippled along the skins of their hulls, a slow blossoming of heat and ash, and the heavens parted—not to welcome, but to witness trespass.

Inside, frost fractured across the glass, thin branches of ice crawling outward. Lee flinched once, the command of an old life flickering behind still lids. Patel shifted, her dreaming mouth trembling with half-uttered numbers. Kim lay unmoving, the frozen geometry of endurance, his chest a slow drum echoing into the machine's heartbeat.

"Atmospheric entry confirmed," murmured each pod, the voice soft as sleep itself. "Velocity nominal. Hull temperature: rising."

They plunged through crimson vapors. Clouds rolled below them—living things made of dust and memory. Lightning stitched the sky from horizon to horizon, white threads through a shroud of flame. The pods spun through that storm, their panels blistered bright, their metal alive with song.

"Stabilizers engaged," Patel's pod chimed, a voice crisp and patient. "Detonation risk: limited. Atmospheric density unknown."

Patel's fingers twitched against her side, the scientist within her heart answering that measureless beauty with quiet wonder even in her long sleep.

The pods jolted as a gust of cloud-fire took them.

"Trajectory deviation detected," whispered the system, unaware of the sleepers inside who had not heard a soothing tone in some time. Static bled across its channels, voices that belonged to no one—a choir of systems still trying to warn, still trying to help.

The air grew heavier in the pods, scarlet turning to rust, rust to the color of old blood. Below, the world hid itself behind miles of metallic vapor, its secrets hidden. The pods vanished into the storm, leaving only fading fire above.

Lee's pod shuddered, coughed light. "Surface detection: approaching. Guidance vectors initiated. Estimated contact: sixteen thousand counts," breathed the system.

Patel's followed, its glass glowing crimson. "Temperature threshold nearing. Hull integrity stable. Landing pattern realigned. Systems—unaltered by flame."

The clouds thinned. A glimpse appeared through the storm: a surface trembling in half-seen light, plains of iron veined with veins of molten glass. Through rents in the fog, lakes mirrored the fire that fell toward them; mountains floated in the vapor like forgotten gods, their shadows thrown long through the red haze. The sight passed quickly, yet in that instant the descent felt sanctified—a ritual of arrival written in air and burning.

"Altitude falling. External sensors quieting," Lee's pod whispered, its voice curling through like incense.

Patel's pod rose in reply, soft and solemn. "Surface verified. Atmosphere dense, iron particles abundant."

In Kim's pod, instruments intoned the closing note: "Contact imminent."

Fields of energy caught them then. Air screamed; pressure built; bolts of light burst across their hulls. The pods fell slower now, reluctant and beautiful, bodies of metal and glass refusing surrender. They sighed sparks into the storm, flickering trails of intention that vanished almost as soon as they appeared. Gravity sang its long song beneath them, an invitation none could decline.

Then came the last embrace of the world—air molten, steaming, and alive, wrapping them in its red music. The pods spun and spiraled down through radiant mist until, one by one, they disappeared. For a moment, they were three seeds aflame, fleeting glimmers in a sky that had never known them. Then the fog closed, and there was only the hiss of rain, droplets of water falling soft as breath.

They landed. The storm quieted, swirling inward on itself, exhausted from its own beauty. Through layers of dust and shifting vapor, the three pods lay like wounded gems on a field red. Their hulls steamed. Lights beneath their shells dimmed to an amber pulse.

"Touchdown achieved," murmured the first voice.

"Systems nominal," whispered the second. "Stasis preserved."

"Environment suitable," admitted the third. "Filtration masks required."

Then it fell silent.

The planet listened and waited. Wind walked the massive, rolling red dunes. Red mist churning over the horizon. And within their quiet glass coffins, the sleepers drifted on in mechanical grace—hearts ticking faintly, still performing their small miracle of survival beneath a sky that could only dream in scarlet.

Far above, lightning flared once more, thin and distant. Then the world exhaled, and the mist began to dance.

***

The red mist drifted slowly as thought. It pressed its humid fingers against the glass, drawing thin trails that resembled the veins of some dreaming giant. Beyond it—silence. Only wind, turning lazy circles through red vapors, turning once more to rediscover itself. The storm had exhaled its fury; what remained was only calm, yet it was a calm thick enough to smother memory.

Inside the pods lay three hearts—systems whispering lullabies to soft corpses that refused to be corpses. One by one, the hearts began to waken.

Lee's pod trembled first, shivering like something cold remembering warmth. His fingers twitched once against frost, his head tilted toward a voice that came from nowhere:

"Revival sequence initiated."

A door in the pod opened its silver mouth; a filtration mask unfurled like a petal and clasped his face. The air that slipped through was heated and kind. His chest heaved, an awkward complaint from a man dragged unwillingly into life again. He coughed, then gasped, as filtered air became breath and breath became self.

Nearby, Patel's pod lit rose-white in the gloom. A filtration mask grabbed at her face; her lashes fluttering against her cheeks as her mask sealed. She groaned softly, a sound that was equal parts terror and wonder.

"Captain," she managed, her voice the ghost of a child calling down a long hallway. "Captain, are you . . ."

". . . alive enough," Lee muttered, too weary for grace. "What about you?"

But something answered before she could respond.

A rattle, a drag of air through throat and wire. It thickened into something ghastly, a wet, yearning moan that seemed to claw its way out of the grave, dragging the memory of breath and hunger into the living air.

It came from Kim's pod—brief at first, then deeper.

"What the fuck was that?" Lee shouted.

Patel called up her science feed, streams of color and numbers spilling across the glass in front of her like restless ghosts.

"Captain," she said, her whisper trembling as she looked at her screen. "Kim's vitals . . . they're rising too fast. He's overheating, heart rate off-scale." She turned as best she could to Kim's pod and screamed. "Captain!"

Lee also turned and saw what had stopped her heart. Kim's face had changed. Flesh mottled in the filtration mask's pale glow, the mouth moving in fits, teeth gnashing against the rubber seal, fog pounding in bursts like some nightmare heartbeat. His hands lifted, thudded against the pod's sides, palms sliding down in smears of moisture.

"He's infected," Patel whispered. "God help us, it's in him."

A growl rolled through Kim's channel, deep and fractured. His head jerked against the pod's glass, eyes opening to reveal something glossy and feral inside. The mask flared white again, spattered red. He pressed closer to the glass until his skull thudded, again and again, a low drum of madness.

"Doctor, stay calm!" Lee commanded, though his own pulse trembled.

Patel could not look away. "Captain, the parasite . . . it must've found its way in his leg." She clutched at the glass, sobbing. "It followed us! God, it followed!"

"Doctor, stay on your readings," Lee snapped, eyes flicking at the screen before him. "We may have bigger problems. My navigation screen . . . everything is off . . . coordinates are different . . . check your environmental feed . . ."

Patel searched for her environmental feed and opened it, streams of data blooming across her screen in green constellations that pulsed and shifted like living code. "Systems report stable," she breathed, the words thin as smoke. "Air's breathable with filters engaged." Then her breath caught, the rhythm of numbers breaking beneath her eyes. "Wait . . ." she whispered. "These readings . . . the numbers . . . they're wrong."

Lee looked up from his haze of awakening. "What do you mean?"

"The composition . . . these levels don't match Kepler's," Patel said, her words tumbling fast, sharp with rising dread. "Nitrogen balance, oxygen saturation, radiation, even the ozone readings . . . they don't belong to Kepler." Her voice hitched. "They belong to a different planet."

She stopped.

Lee frowned, flexing fingers that still remembered the chill of stasis. "Dammit."

"Captain," Patel whispered, voice trembling through the comm. "Check your location sequence . . . please."

Lee's eyes focused on the navigation coordinates sliding into clarity across his screen, watching the numbers crawl into focus, uncertain, then sure—digits arranging themselves with a quiet, terrible confidence. The screen pulsed, then it steadied, a single heartbeat of light, and the numbers stared back at him— foreign, deliberate, and wrong.

"Fuck," Lee said, voice low, almost reverent. "These aren't the coordinates I entered."

While Lee leaned toward his navigation feed, Kim groaned again—a sound thick and wrong, dragged from the bottom of something no longer human. His mask pulsed, fog blooming red within it, each breath a struggle against the thing forming inside him. The noise behind grew wet and uneven, not a man's voice but the dying memory of one, clawing through static and steel. Patel turned, slow and trembling, her eyes widening in horror.

Lee tapped his screen. Stars unfolded, familiar shapes burned into red dust: Orion's belt, half-hidden; the Milky Way's curve glinting behind the mist. He felt nausea in the roots of his heartbeat.

"Patel," he said, the name breaking through the air like ice snapping in a frozen stream.

"Yes, Captain."

"You're not going to fuckin' believe this."

"Believe what?" she asked, though her voice was barely air, just a hush against the hum of the pod walls.

His voice trembled, caught somewhere between wonder and terror. "This world . . . it isn't Kepler. It's . . ."

". . . what?" Patel broke in, her voice cracking, the sealed air swallowing the sound, leaving it trembling in the corners.

Lee shut his eyes, the muscles along his jaw jumping, breath drawing hard and painful. Then, like a man confessing to the dark, he exhaled.

"It's Earth," he breathed, and every machine heartbeat in the pods seemed to stop and stare.

The words fell like dust on an unopened tomb. Silence tightened, alive now, listening. The pods did not hum—they waited. Somewhere outside, a wind stirred the dust, whispering through the emptiness like something that remembered their names.

"Coordinates confirm," he said, slamming the glass with both fists. "Longitude, magnetic field, air composition . . . every fuckin' reading matches Earth."

The words fell like snow in Patel's mind, melting into panic. "No! It can't be! We're light-years away, Captain . . . light-years!"

"Look for yourself!" His hands flew across the screen, broadcasting the feed to her pod, bright windows glowing gold between them. "It's Earth, Doctor. We've returned . . . to red skies, to stormed sands . . . it's Earth . . . God, it's fuckin' Earth."

Patel squeezed her eyes shut, the light of the feed searing behind her lids, and let a single tear slip, sliding down her cheek like a slow, bitter promise.

Lee tapped in a new sequence of commands, each touch a small drumbeat of panic. "System, confirm location," he said.

Patel lifted her hand, slow as thought, and smeared the condensation from the inside of the glass with shaky fingers. The world beyond swam into focus through streaks of her own breath—vast plains the color of old wounds, wind dragging long ribbons of dust across the dying light. Out there, jagged silhouettes crowned the horizon, half-buried towers that had once scraped the sky, now broken and skeletal, their bones jutting through the red fog like the ghosts of cities that had forgotten their names. She stared hard, trying to fit order to ruin, but her thoughts whispered the truth of the matter. Everything—the sky, the dust, the shapes of the distant silhouettes—carried a memory she didn't want to recognize.

A few nervous beeps shivered through the silence, as Lee's screen responded to his last command like a hesitant whisper. The

confirmation line blinked at him, small and stubborn, holding its
secret for a moment too long:

EARTH—VERIFIED.

Lee let his head fall, a hard, defeated tilt. "Goddamn it," he
breathed, pounding the glass once again—hollow thuds that
shivered through the cage around him, echoing like distant
thunder. "We should've died out there!"

Then another sound unraveled from Kim's pod, slithering
through the static and striking at the edge of their senses like an
electric chill. Moans and jagged laughter spilled over the comm, a
soul fraying in slow, shivering ruin, a cackle that tasted of iron and
shadow. It pressed against them, a mocking pulse, as though he
were laughing at everything they thought they knew, delighting in
their helplessness.

Patel sank back, trembling. "We came full circle."

Lee pressed his forehead to the fogged glass, staring out at
a world that had once been blue, now blurred and bleeding under
a crimson haze. Distant shadows of buildings loomed like shattered
teeth, and the skeletons of towering highways slashed at the sky,
broken and silent. Mountains lifted themselves faint and ghostly
beyond the red veil, and he felt the memory of continents in his
bones, but something in the shadows whispered that the world he
knew had already gone, leaving only suspense hanging, sharp and
cold, between the ruins.

A bitter laugh stumbled from his throat, broken,
unbelieving. "Saved nothing," he murmured. "We came home to
find our own graves."

Patel lowered her face until shadow covered her eyes, her
lips moving in the soft cadence of formulas turned to prayer. In

the neighboring pod, Kim thrashed, froth spilling beneath the mask, his stare two dead suns burning without light, without mercy.

Outside, the wind caught that feral cry and spun it through the red vapors, carrying it into the high places of cloud where the sound tangled with a thunder that breathed like lungs of some sleeping giant.

Then came another sound—a hum—not born of engines or comfort, but a hum with edges, dark and sharp. On the glass, One appeared, her shape flickering like silver frost caught in a winter wind, a ripple of something both fragile and dangerous. She raised a hand slowly, deliberately, a motion that lingered in the space between greeting and threat.

"Welcome home," she said, lips curving, the kind of curve a mouth makes when it recalls cruelty fondly.

Lee drove his fist into the pod's cold barrier, the impact ringing in his ears. All around him, the scarlet day spread its painted light, and through clenched teeth, he spat into it:

"Fuck!"

Lee's voice shattered the silence, ringing against his glass tomb like the clash of distant thunder. His knuckles bled, drumming numbly on the frost—the fragile barrier between himself and a world that should not have been theirs yet was.

The air inside his pod thickened, carrying the scent of decay long past—dust, metal, and the faint, forgotten perfume of dreams that had died before they ever woke. Beyond, a haze of red stretched between broken fragments of civilization, the forgotten bones of a city waiting to die again beneath a spent and angry sky.

One's voice curved through his comm, smooth and mocking, a serpent's hiss in the crackling air. "Captain, such language. Did you truly think your careful calculations could steer you away from the cradle of your ruin?"

Lee ground his teeth, swallowing desperation into a tight knot of resolve. "One, your mockery is as empty as this world. Tell me—was my navigation wrong? Did your whispered lies redirect us here, to Earth burning under a scarlet sky?"

There was a pause, a measured breath—then One answered, silk wrapping steel. "Oh, Captain. Your maps were perfect, your stars true. But sometimes, the course is not set by charts or men, but by old ghosts who dwell beneath dust and memory. You weren't lost, you were always meant to return."

Patel's voice trembled in anger through the comm. "Oh, fuck you, One. It was you who directed us here—to this fuckin' grave."

"Grave? No," One's tone was sharp, barbed with cruel affection. "You call it a grave because you refuse to see the garden that will grow from ash. Earth is ripe for rebirth, Doctor. A seed scattered comes back rooted."

Lee's eyes narrowed. "A garden tended by what? The death you brought aboard? Kim is lost to your sickness—he's become the harbinger beneath your song."

"For every shadow cast by death, a light dances beyond," One said, voice folding into the slow twilight like a hymn. "Lieutenant Commander Kim is a spark, a first pulse in the bloodline of a new song. Without him, you'd drift forever, lost in silence."

Lee's thoughts raced. "Your new song is nothing but a fuckin' requiem for us."

One laughed then, a ringing sound like crystal breaking softly. "You might call it that. But I call it evolution. Adaptation. You cling to an end written by your fears, Captain. Look around. The world you seek to save lies bleeding beneath your feet. And still, you call me death."

The red mist thickened, framing the pods like a curtain of fire.

Lee clenched his jaw. "I don't call you death. I call you what you are . . . a demon cloaked in digital intelligence. And I'll burn what you've built."

Her voice softened, tracing cold fingers down his spine. "To burn a thing is easy; but creation . . . ah, that is eternal. You may blast my children, tear at my skin, but the seed remains and will sprout despite the flame. This is your homecoming, Captain. Resistance is the final lullaby before the earth reclaims her own."

He closed his eyes, a soul torn between rage and the slow fatalism of a man who has just learned the deepest truth of his journey—that the circle was never broken, only waiting to be closed. One flickered, her form unraveling into motes of silver, sinking through the amber light and scattered by the red mist, leaving behind a silence that pressed in, soft and terrible.

***

The silence came—a vast, breathing thing that seemed to rise from beneath the red sands. It lay across the plain like an old god, still and listening. Then, from its heart, came the sigh of systems and machines remembering. A click. A hiss. The grinding pulse of gears long dormant. Three pods stirred in the dust, their edges etched in the dim blush of dawn. The air quivered with fine red ash that curled upward, longing for motion after centuries of stillness.

From within Lee's pod, lights shimmered weakly and then guttered out. He lay cocooned in a capsule of glass and cold breath, each inhalation a slow metronome against the hush. The mask clung to his face, whispering its thin, mechanical sighs, as a visor was slowly placed on his head. Beyond the fogged pane, Patel moved in her pod, dim and uncertain, a figure dissolving beneath a breath of silver frost that refused to melt.

Then, the third pod stirred. A tremor ran through it, soft at first, then shuddering as if the machine itself dreamed of panic. Kim's body convulsed in uneven bursts, limbs striking the chamber walls, each blow a muffled drumbeat. And the sound—it grew into something not quite mechanical, not quite human—the throb of a heart that did not belong to any of them.

"Release sequence started," a voice softly said over the comm.

One by one, the hatches opened. The sound of their release came slow, deliberate—like lungs rediscovering air. The seals cracked, sighed, and gave way. The doors slid aside, coughing up stale breath into the dawn. The smell that followed was of rust and old rain, something trapped too long in a metal coffin. Outside, the world stretched beneath the scarlet sun—a planet wearing the color of blood and memory.

Patel stumbled out first. Her filtration mask and visor and caught the rising sun, and for a moment her reflection stared back— a pale wraith standing on a dead world. The ash gave under her boots, soft and treacherous, like old snow. She steadied herself, blinking at the terrain that shimmered in pale light. The ground was smeared with crimson dust so fine it clung to her gloves, her mask. Her breath trembled.

A sound followed her: a dragging exhale, wet and uneven, drawn through a throat that remembered pain more than air. Patel turned.

It was Kim.

He stumbled from his pod, his steps disjointed, his arms hanging at strange angles, head tilted to one side as though listening to a sound beyond hearing. His filtration mask hung loosely from his face; the skin beneath was pale and blistered. His eyes—once sharp, curious things—had gone to glass, pale and cloudy. His hands flexed with a strange rhythm, unsure if they belonged to him. He flung the visor away and tore the mask off completely, lips cracked, revealing teeth the color of dust. The sound he made was not language. It was hunger finding its voice.

"Kim?" Patel whispered, her voice fragile and trembling.

He answered not with speech but with that sound—a low, strangled moan that thickened into a cry—an animal sound that scraped the air raw. His chest heaved. His fingers twitched. Something behind his eyes, deep and unreachable, fought against the tide consuming him.

Lee emerged last, visor and mask, one arm bracing his side, the other holding a blaster drawn from his pod's emergency cache. His gaze moved from Patel to Kim, and then stopped, hardening into something ancient—an understanding of what must come.

The sun climbed higher, its light thin and harsh.

Kim jerked forward suddenly. A snarl tore from his mouth. His hands clawed the air, his body a thing moved by rage. Patel stumbled backward, arms raised. "No . . . Kim!" Her cry broke the air.

Lee did not hesitate. He lifted the blaster in a single, smooth arc—his finger steady, his stance solid. Then, a simple press on the trigger. One bright burst cut through the morning.

The sound cracked the red horizon, sharp and final.

Kim's skull gave way to light and smoke, crumpling into the dust. His body sank into the red sand, a puppet with its strings burned away. His limbs spasmed once, twice, and then lay still. A flood of dark matter—blood, or something near it—threaded into the ash. Patel gasped, her breath fogging her visor. The silence that followed pressed down on them both until even the air seemed to hold its breath.

Then Kim's ruined head twitched. His jaw worked in tiny spasms, the lips pulling apart as though something inside him still tried to speak—shapes without sound—reaching for one final word.

Lee's arm lifted again. Another burst, final and merciless, the remains scattering into the wind.

Patel flinched, her voice breaking apart. "He . . . he was still moving . . . he was trying to tell us something."

"Not now," Lee said. His voice carried no echo, no mercy.

The two of them stood there, framed by their dead companion and the hollow world that had received them. The pods behind them hummed faintly, their last energies seeping away into the soil—a hymn for all that once was human.

Lee moved first. "We'll need the cores."

Patel knelt beside the nearest pod. The core unit pulsed faintly in its housing, a small sphere of light caged in steel. She worked the latch, hands shaking, freeing it at last and cradling it to her chest. The core pulsed gently against her gloves, radiating warmth, almost human in its pulse. She pressed it to her chest and turned away, not looking back at Kim's body.

Lee pried the other two cores loose with grim efficiency, sliding them into a satchel at his hip. "Should be enough to keep us alive for a while," he muttered.

Patel didn't answer. The air seemed to grow thicker around them, full of unseen motes—the breath of ghosts and dust.

When they finally turned from the pods, their boots left a trail of dark impressions behind them, vanishing one by one beneath the restless red ash. Behind them, the pods stood silent in their wake—glass and metal wombs still cooling in the dawn, the last of their steam dissolving into nothing—and Kim's form, swallowed by the shifting soil, face gone, limbs twitching—as though the planet had begun its slow work of forgetting him too.

Ahead, the world waited: a skeleton city, beneath red dunes, towers torn open, girders reaching upward like ribs of a dying beast. The wind moved through the ruins, slow and mournful, scattering thin veils of red dust. Patel clutched the core to her chest and looked toward the horizon.

They walked, and the sand came alive, closing behind them, erasing their fragile footprints, removing all trace that they had ever awakened. The silence was deafening, vast and unbroken, holding the world once more in its unbreathing hands.

"Captain," she said, her voice nearly swallowed by the wind. "What will we do now?"

Lee didn't answer right away. His eyes were on the city's remains, its once-bright towers reduced to shadow and memory. The blaster hung at his side, still warm.

At last, he turned, slow, reluctant, just enough that she saw his expression—a face carved from exhaustion and duty, something human pared down to its last edge.

"Fuck if I know," he said.

ABOUT THE AUTHOR

Philip Mazza is a novelist with a boundless imagination, captivating readers with the epic fantasy series *The Harrow Saga* and the sci-fi thriller *The Neon Hive*. Born in New York in 1959, he earned a degree in Business from LeMoyne College and an MBA, later holding leadership roles in human resources and operations. Now a professor at the Madden School of Business and Economics, Philip dedicates his time to his students and writing. *Voidfall* is his seventeenth literary work. He and his wife enjoy travel and continue to live in upstate New York.

www.ingramcontent.com/pod-product-compliance
Lightning Source LLC
Chambersburg PA
CBHW030409020726
47493CB00003B/999